Summerdog

Novelization
by
THOM ROBERTS

Based on the Screenplay by
George and Sherry LaFollette Zabriskie.

AN AVON CAMELOT BOOK

SUMMERDOG is an original publication of Avon Books.
This work has never before appeared in book form.

AVON BOOKS
A division of
The Hearst Corporation
959 Eighth Avenue
New York, New York 10019

Original screenplay copyright © 1978
by Louis Santi Publishing
"Running Free" and "Hobo and Me" copyright © 1977
Nothing Ventured Company
Photographs copyright © 1977 The Zabriskies
and Terry Bisbee
Published by arrangement with the author and
Louis Santi Publishing.
Library of Congress Catalog Card Number: 77-93665
ISBN: 0-380-01950-7

First Camelot Printing, February, 1978

CAMELOT TRADEMARK REG. U.S. PAT. OFF. AND IN
OTHER COUNTRIES, MARCA REGISTRADA, HECHO EN
U.S.A.

Printed in the U.S.A.

Table of Contents

THOM ROBERTS has written several books and many short stories for young people. A former editor for *Humpty Dumpty's Magazine*, he is currently writing their book reviews, and he is an instructor for The Institute of Children's Literature. He is the editor of two Avon books: THE HOLLOW TREE and THE SNOWED-IN BOOK. He also builds houses out of recycled materials and lives with his family in Woodstock, New York.

I

Becky Norman stood anxiously on the front stoop of the dingy old apartment building. She was waiting for her father to drive up in their car.

The building had once been elegant with fresh white paint, handsome black shutters, and Victorian curlicues along the roof line. Even when Becky's mother and father had moved there, and when her older brother, Adam, had been born nearly twelve years ago, the building had had dignity. But then Mr. and Mrs. Baleeka bought it, and it began to look tired and feeble, just as people do when there's no one around to care.

But still, Becky thought, the building wasn't all that bad. All of the apartments had beautiful, heavy, carved oak doors with brass knobs and knockers. Many of the apartments themselves proved that some people still cared for the old building.

The Normans' apartment was one of these. It was on the top floor, and there was a skylight that let in plenty of light for both plants and people. The walls were freshly painted and decorated with pictures Becky and Adam had drawn and painted over the years. Solid old pine furniture, a heavy stuffed sofa, and colorful hand-braided rugs added to the warmth of their four rooms.

Becky was going to help her father pack the car. As she waited, she talked to an armload of dolls and stuffed animals. "Boy, it's gonna be neat living in the country all summer. We can swim every day and have tea parties, and . . . Hey, where's Sasha?" She dropped the dolls and animals to the stoop and looked for her stuffed rabbit. Sasha, who slept with her every night, and who had always done so, wasn't there. "Sasha!"

A beat-up, medium-sized green hatchback car pulled up in front of the building, and Peter, Becky's father, double-parked. As he did, Becky yelled, "Popi! It's Sasha! I can't find Sasha!"

"Wait a minute," Peter yelled from the car. "I can't hear you." He got out and went to the stoop where Becky was standing, surrounded by the dolls and animals.

"I can't find Sasha!" Becky cried.

"He'll turn up," Peter said. He went past her and into the dark, gloomy lobby where there was a pile of suitcases, sleeping bags, and duffel bags. "Don't worry, honey. We'll find him," he said. "Now we have to get the car loaded. I'll help you later."

8

"But Popi!" Becky followed him to the car.

Her father began tying the luggage to the rack on top of the car. As he tossed the end of the rope over the car and went to the street side, he said, "Becky, I've got to get this stuff loaded, or we'll never get out of here."

"Popi!" wailed Becky again. She followed him to the other side of the car. "It's Sasha!"

A blue van behind them honked. "Get inside!" Peter ordered. "How many times have I told you never to come to the street side of the car!" He opened the door and shoved her inside. As he did, the van honked again.

"Hey, buddy," yelled the van driver. "Shut your door. Think you own the street!" Cars behind the van honked, too. "You're blocking the whole street!"

Peter slammed the door and flattened himself against the car as the van and then a taxi drove by, uncomfortably close.

"Popi, wait," said Becky through the open window.

"Becky, I don't have time now. Where's your mother? Go back inside and ask her to help you find Sasha. Where is she anyway? We've got a six-hour drive ahead of us, and she's supposed to be bringing down the rest of the stuff with Adam."

Becky started to get out of the car, again on the street side, and Peter yelled, "Becky, the other side! The curb side!"

Becky got out on the other side and said, "Okay, I'll go ask her, but she'll be mad, too. She's writing letters."

"Letters!" Peter muttered, stepping back from the car. "How can she be writing letters? We've got to get out . . ." A car honked, and the driver slammed on the brakes. "Darn!" said Peter. "Go on. Get Adam to help you find Sasha."

"But Popi, my other animals and . . ."

"Don't worry. I'll put them in back. You go up and find Sasha, and tell your mother to get moving."

"Okay." Becky went back inside. After she pushed the elevator button, she said, "That'll take forever," and she ran up the stairs to the fourth floor.

When she got inside the apartment, her mother was still sitting at her cluttered desk, typing a letter. Before Becky could say anything, Adam came into the room. He had sandy blond hair, as Becky and his mother did, and was wearing a red bandanna on his forehead.

"Mom, I can't find my fishing rod. I've looked everywhere. I've got to bring it, and I can't find it."

Carol Norman, continuing to type, said, "Did you look in the back of your closet? I mean way back, under everything?"

"Yup," Adam said.

"Under your bed?"

"Uh-huh."

"Mumma," Becky interrupted as Carol paused.

"Wait a minute, Becky. Adam, did you look on top of your bookcase?"

"Yup," Adam said, shrugging and stuffing his hands into his blue-jean pockets.

Carol stopped typing, and then she said, "I know where it is. I saw it. It's with the Christmas tree stuff at the top of the coat closet. All the once-in-a-while stuff is there."

"Hey, great," said Adam as he turned toward the hall where the coat closet was. "Thanks, Mom."

"Mumma," Becky said, "I can't find Sasha."

"Hold on, dear," Carol said. "Adam, before you climb up there—and do be careful—I want you to take this note down to the superintendent's apartment. Give it to Bill. It's about watering the plants."

As she handed the envelope to Adam, Becky glanced at the potted avocado tree behind her mother's desk and at the spider plant hanging in the window.

"Aw, Mom, can't I get the rod first and then deliver the note?"

"Adam, please. You've got the note in your hand. Do this first." Adam turned to go, and she said, "And while you're downstairs, you might as well take the cosmetic kit. Tell your father I'll be ready in just a few minutes."

As Adam went out the door, she called after him. "And Adam, if Bill's not there, leave the note with the Baleekas, our *dear* landlords."

"Those creeps," muttered Adam as the door slammed.

"Mumma," Becky said as Carol turned back to the typewriter. "Sasha's lost. Popi says you should help find him."

"Well, I can't right this minute. Did you look in the back of your closet? I mean *way* back, under all that stuff?"

"Uh-huh."

"On top of your bookcase?"

"Yup."

"Under your bed?"

"Uh-huh."

Carol tugged thoughtfully at a strand of hair and said, "Wait a minute! I saw that rabbit somewhere this very morning. I know! That silly animal of yours was munching on the philodendron."

"Hey, thanks, Mumma." Becky ran to the other side of the room and found the stuffed, love-worn rabbit propped up behind the potted philodendron plant. She held Sasha close to her face and said, "I wish you were real."

"Sure," her mother said sarcastically. "That's just what we need around here, a bunch of live rabbits. No thank you, not in a city apartment."

Becky, still hugging Sasha, went over to the desk and said, "I was just wishing, that's all."

"Okay, little lady blue-eyes, I happen to like Sasha just the way he is, even if he is old and lumpy and scruffy. Now that you've found him, why don't you wait in the car. Tell your father I forgot about the proposal to save the dolphins, and I won't be able to live with myself if I don't get these letters off to Congress before we go."

"Okay, Mumma." Becky went out. When she got to the first floor, she saw Adam knocking on the Baleekas' door, and she slipped by quietly, without being seen.

Adam knocked again, and then he heard a shrill voice from inside the apartment. "Is that you, Bill?"

"No, Mrs. Baleeka. It's me, Adam Norman. I've got a note for Bill about watering the plants while we're

12

away. But he's not home, and Mom said to leave it with you."

"That no-good super," said the unpleasant voice, still from behind the door. "I don't know why Mr. Baleeka keeps him on. And you people—troublemaking all the time. We're landlords, not servants!"

"Here we go again," muttered Adam. Then he yelled, "Yes, I know, I know, Mrs. Baleeka. But please, just this once, could I leave this note for Bill? It's got money in it."

Mrs. Baleeka opened the door slightly and stuck her pudgy hand out. "I don't know why we're so good to you people," she grumbled, snatching the envelope.

Just as she grabbed it, a small black poodle, wearing a pink bow, ran out through the crack.

"Gigi! Precious!"

Adam ran down the hall after the dog and scooped her up in his arms. As he brought her back to the Baleekas' door, he hugged and petted her. "Good dog," he said as Gigi licked him in the face. "Good Gigi, nice Gigi. I sure wish we could have a dog."

"Well, you can't," snapped Mrs. Baleeka as she opened the door. "It's in your lease. No pets!"

As Adam handed Gigi to her, he saw Mr. Baleeka step into the living room. He approached the open door and said, "What's goin' on here?"

Adam noticed he was wearing a shoulder holster with a pistol in it.

"Gee, Mr. Baleeka, is that a *real* gun?"

Mr. Baleeka glared at him. "Naw, it's just a toy, sonny boy." Mrs. Baleeka slammed the door.

As Adam turned toward the elevator, he heard Mr. Baleeka yell, "Stupid! You'd open our door to anybody."

"I thought it was Bill," Adam heard Mrs. Baleeka say.

"Dummy, that kid don't sound like Bill."

Adam waited for the elevator and stared at an eviction notice on the door of another apartment. When he got upstairs, his mother was still at her desk, typing. "Hey!" he yelled, out of breath. "Mom! Hey, Mom! Did you know Mr. Baleeka carries a real gun?"

Without looking up, Carol said, "No, but I'm not surprised. He's just the type."

"But, Mom," Adam said, disappointed at her reaction, "you hate guns."

Carol stopped typing and said, "Yes, I do. I'm not fond of Mr. Baleeka, either. But, Adam, a lot of people keep guns these days. It makes them feel safer, somehow. It makes me feel the opposite." She faced him. "I take it Bill wasn't in."

"No," Adam said. "But Mom, Dad's furious. He says he can't get one more thing in the car. And that this is one heck of a time to catch up on your correspondence!"

"Adam, watch your tone of voice!"

"It's not mine. It's Dad's." Trying to hold back a grin, he said, "I'm gonna get my rod now and take it down to the car."

"Okay. Tell your father I'll be down in a minute."

Adam found the fishing rod in the coat closet, and then he hurried downstairs. Peter was standing on the street side of the car again, tying the cosmetic kit to the mound of luggage already on the rack. Becky was

14

on the curb side, shouting, "I said, Mumma says she can't live without some kind of fish or somethin'."

"Oh," said Peter with a confused expression on his face. "Yeah. Well, thank you, Becky, for the message. It clears everything up."

"You're welcome, Popi," Becky yelled as a motorcycle roared past.

"Dad, Dad!" Adam ran to the street side of the car. "Here. Here's my rod. Can you tie it on top? I've got to mail Mom's letters." He ran down the street toward the mailbox.

Peter muttered to himself and tied the rod to the side of the rack. "I knew we should have hired a moving van," he said, winking at Becky.

As he said it, Carol came out of the building, carrying the potted avocado tree. When she got to the car, she said, "I know it seems foolish, but. . . ."

"But nothing!" Peter shouted. "Carol, look at this mess! There's no room. You simply can't put that tree in this car."

"Please, Peter. I know the philodendron and the spider plants and the cactus will make it through the summer, no matter what Bill does, but the avocado's different. It needs loving care."

"So do I," Peter said, sighing. "Look, Carol, it's simply a matter of space. There *is* no space. Look at this car! There's hardly room for us."

"I know, I know, but we'll make room. The avocado's special. We raised it from a pit, remember? You're the one who started it, with those toothpicks and the jar. We can't leave it now."

"Oh, okay," he said, taking the tree from her. He opened the door on the passenger side and placed the pot on the floor. "We'll take it, but it goes on your side. You're going to have to cope with it for the next six hours. And I make no promises about its survival."

Becky giggled as her mother slipped into the car. The avocado foliage almost hid her. As Peter pushed more foliage inside and shut the door, he said, "What's this Becky tells me about fish? We're not taking any fish with us."

Carol brushed leaves away from her face and said, "Fish. What fish? What did Becky say? Oh, I know. It's the proposal to protect dolphins from the tuna fishermen. I promised I'd write Congress."

Adam ran up to the car, and he and Becky got in the back, where they were surrounded by dolls, stuffed animals, extra blankets, and sleeping bags. Peter got into the driver's seat and said, "Letters to Congress?" He grinned and added, "I should have known." He put the key in the ignition, and there was a loud buzz. "Fasten your seat belt," he said.

"It is fastened," Carol said.

"Well, so's mine. Check yours again. It mustn't be quite right."

Fighting off avocado leaves, Carol unbuckled and rebuckled her belt. "It's as good as I can get it."

The buzzer was still buzzing. Peter unbuckled and rebuckled his belt. "Forget dolphins!" he yelled. "Get Congress to do something about these stupid buzzers!"

"How can you say that?" Carol said indignantly.

Suddenly the buzzing stopped, and Peter said, "Okay,

nobody touch anything. Our systems are all *go*, at last."
He turned the key, and the car started.

"Hooray! Hooray!" Becky shouted. "At last we're
on our way!"

"Goodbye, city. Hello, country," Adam said. "Here
we go!"

2

Once they were out of town and on the highway, Carol finally found a compromise position with the avocado tree. Adam and Becky only had to stop twice to go to the bathroom, and even with the stops, the seat belt buzzer went crazy only once. Peter figured out how to disconnect the fuse so it couldn't happen again. Becky and Adam argued some about who was on whose side in the back seat, but finally Becky made a tent out of a blanket and sat under it for most of the last two hours of the drive.

When it seemed they would never get there, Becky yelled from her tent. "Boy, it sure is taking us a long time!"

"Yeah," Adam said. "How much longer is it going to be?"

"I don't know," Peter answered. "Maybe half an hour to the town."

"Whew! It's about time," Adam said. "It's so crowded I've got cramps on my cramps."

They turned off the highway and onto a narrow country road that wound through lush, rolling hills. Becky took her tent down, and both she and Adam admired the green meadows where sheep and cows were grazing lazily under massive oak and maple trees. The sky was clear, and the country air was fresh and sweet. "Boy, this sure beats the city," Adam said as they crossed over an old covered bridge."

"You don't see many bridges like that any more," Peter said.

"Why do we have to live in the city anyway?" Becky asked. "If we lived in the country all the time, Sasha could be real."

"What?" Peter glanced at her in the mirror. "How could Sasha . . ."

"Never mind," Carol interrupted. "It's something Becky and I discussed earlier."

"You're talking in code again. I should have known."

Twenty or thirty minutes later Carol pointed and said, "Look, there's that funny little general store we saw when we were up here in March."

"Yeah, great," Peter said, pulling in front of the old whitewashed wooden building. "We can get provisions here and ask the storekeeper how to get to the house."

"You don't remember?" Adam asked.

"Yeah, but not exactly," his father answered. "I'll know with a little reminder."

Becky and Adam got out through the hatchback, and Peter helped Carol move the avocado so she could get out. They left the tree by the side of the car when they went inside the store.

"Hi, there," Peter said to the man behind the counter. "Beautiful day."

"Yup." The man stood up and regarded the family curiously.

They got the groceries they needed, and after they'd been put into bags, the storekeeper said, "Ya got a lotta groceries there. Stayin' fer the summer, eh?" He twisted the ends of his long mustache.

"Yeah, all summer," Becky said. "Popi's writing a book about old iron furnaces."

"Ya don't say. Well, ya come to the right place." Turning to Carol, he said, "Ma'am, I better help you with one of those bags."

Loaded with grocery bags, they all walked out to the car, and after they'd packed them around the kids in the back, the storekeeper stared at the tree and said, "Ya gonna leave that or the missus here?"

Peter laughed and said, "She's got a system." He helped Carol into the car and handed her the tree.

"Yep," said the storekeeper. "You folks from the city always got systems. Where ya stayin'?"

"At the Bristol place," Peter said. "Can you tell us how to get there?"

"Reckon I can. You mean the *bottle* house. Everybody knows where that is." He scratched his head. "Now, Jethro's dairy barn's about, oh, maybe five miles down the blacktop. Jest the other side there's a dirt road. Take it. 'Bout a mile or so further on—but before ya get to Widow Starkey's place—there's a fork. Take the right. Now ya keep straight on till ya come to the new bridge over Wasanooksik Brook. Cross the bridge, take yer first left, and you're there. Ya can't miss it."

"Uh, sure, right," Peter said as he got into the car. "I remember the brook, but . . . You see, we've only seen the place once before when Mr. Wicker—you know, the realtor—showed it to us."

The storekeeper frowned and said, "Wicker took ya, eh? He tell ya 'bout yer neighbor, Caleb Grimes?"

"Caleb Grimes?" Peter said.

"Trapper. Lives up in the backwoods by yer place. Strange one, that Caleb. Well," he said, squinting into the late afternoon sun, "lots of luck. Sure hope I see you folks again."

Carol frowned back at him and said, "Well, I certainly do, too!"

"Thanks," Peter said. "Thanks for the directions."

"Don't mention it," said the storekeeper.

As Peter started the car, Adam said, "He sure talks funny, doesn't he."

"Shush," his mother said. "That's real country talk. It's what he said, not the way he said it, that worries me. Dairy barns, widow's places, unpronounceable brooks, strange trappers . . . Peter, do you honestly have *any* idea how to get there from here?"

"Well," he said, turning back onto the blacktop road,

"his directions were reasonably clear. You *do* remember what he said, don't you?"

"Not a word." She frowned behind the avocado leaves.

"Okay. We'll figure it out. One by one. Down the blacktop to Jethro's dairy barn, right?"

"Right," Carol said. "Five miles, more or less, give or take a few. And how do we know Jethro's place from his neighbors'? You've seen one dairy barn, you've seen 'em all."

" 'Cause his has a dirt road just the other side of it. Hey, look! Just like he said."

A few hundred feet ahead they saw a dairy barn, and beyond it there was a dirt road.

"Hmmm," Carol muttered. "But we've only gone three point eight miles from the store."

"So . . . he's a little off."

Carol thought for a moment as Peter slowed down. Then she said, "You don't suppose there's another barn, by another dirt road, at five miles?"

"No, I'm sure this is the place."

"Why don't we just ask? You know, just to make sure this is the Jethro place."

"Carol, I said I'm sure!" He turned onto the dirt road.

She peered through the leaves and said, "Tell me something, Peter. Why won't you ever ask? What is it, some kind of macho thing?"

"I'm just sure this is right, that's all." He continued on down the dirt road until he came to a fork. "Here's the fork, but where's the Widow Starkey's place? It couldn't be this wreck," he said, pointing to an abandoned shack.

"About a mile or so, down the road," Carol said with sarcasm in her voice. "That's what the man said. We've gone almost three miles. Maybe we've taken the wrong road. But then, you were *so* sure."

Annoyed, Peter said, "I am sure. I mean, this road *does* look familiar . . . don't you think?"

Becky frowned at Adam and said, "See, I told you we're lost!"

"What are you, an eight-year-old fortune teller? Dad knows what he's doing, don't you, Dad?"

Peter took the right fork and said, "Of course. The man said take the right, so we'll take the right. It does look very familiar."

"Sure, Peter, sure," Carol said. "The only time we've been here was in March, and the whole place was covered with snow. But I'm so glad you're so sure. I'm glad you're sure because it's late, and it's going to be dark soon."

Peter stopped the car suddenly, and they all got out.

"Look," Carol said, "all I'm suggesting is we go back to the barn and ask!"

"Okay, okay," Peter grumbled. "But first we've got to figure out how to get back to the barn."

Becky pointed to some wild flowers by a wood line, off to one side of the road, and said, "Oh, could I go pick those flowers, Mumma? Please?"

"Sure, honey. Just don't go far. You could get lost in those woods."

"Want to come, Adam?"

Summerdog

"Naw. I just want to go fishing."

Peter glared at his son. "Later, Adam, later." He turned to Carol and said, "Now, let's be logical about this." He picked up a stick and started to scratch a rough map in the dirt road, as Becky ran into the woods. "We turned off the blacktop at Jethro's barn, right?"

"Maybe," Carol said. "Maybe Jethro's barn, maybe not."

"Well, anyway, we turned off . . ."

"Where's Becky?" Carol interrupted.

"She's all right. Just in the woods picking flowers." Peter pointed at the map in the dirt again.

As Becky continued to pick flowers, she saw something move in the tall grass. It was a fox stalking some unseen prey. "Here, boy, come here." She held out her hand. "Don't be afraid."

Suddenly there was a shot, and the fox ran away into the woods. Becky screamed.

"Becky! Becky!" yelled her parents. They ran toward Becky who was running back from the woods.

"Becky! Becky! What happened, honey?" Peter picked her up and held her.

"Baby! My baby!" Carol cried. "Are you all right?"

Adam looked toward the woods and said, "Who fired at you, Becky? Where is he?"

Carol took Becky from Peter's arms, and as she did, a big man, with a scraggy black beard, and wearing a dirty red and black checked shirt, came out of the woods, carrying a rifle. "You stupid child! You spoiled my shot. Calling to a fox!" He glared at Peter and said, "Listen,

24

mister, you'd better pay me for that pelt your kid made me lose. Fox like that brings a pretty fair price nowadays." He turned to Becky again and said, "You dumb, stupid child!"

"Listen, mister, what's-your-name . . ." Carol began.

"Grimes, lady, Caleb Grimes."

"I don't care what it is," she said, "but don't you speak that way. You could have hurt her!"

"Or worse," Peter said. "I thought country people knew how to handle guns. You could have killed our little girl!"

"City folk, huh?" muttered Grimes. "I should have figured. Just shows how much you know. I only hit what I aim at. I aimed to hit that fox, and I would have, 'cept she spoiled it." He stared furiously at Becky again.

The family, with Becky between her parents, walked slowly back to the car.

"You let her alone, you fool!" Peter yelled. "You've frightened her enough!"

"Yeah," said Adam, suddenly feeling courageous. "Why don't you pick on someone your own size?"

Carol turned and said, "I think you really enjoy killing beautiful little animals."

Caleb ignored her and said to Peter, "Where ya from? You ain't lost now, are ya?"

"Well, not exactly. We rented this house for the summer, and . . ."

Carol interrupted. "But now we can't find it. Yes, we are lost. You wouldn't happen to know where the Bristol house is, would you?"

Caleb Grimes ignored her again and said, "City folk! Ha! Why do you folks come up here where you don't belong?"

"Listen, mister," Peter said, "we've got as much right to be here as you do." He turned to Adam and Becky and said, "Get in the car, kids." Then, to Caleb Grimes, he said, "Thanks for your help, not to mention the scare you've given our family."

Carol helped Adam and Becky into the hatchback, and then as she climbed in with the avocado tree, she said, "We love the country. We love the things that live here in the wild—the flowers and the animals. And we intend to have a good experience here."

"Some experience!" said Adam.

"Yeah?" grumbled Caleb. "Well, maybe that'll learn ya something next time. Will tell ya one thing, though. At least yer headed in the right direction." He laughed and spit a wad of chewing tobacco in the direction of the car.

"Delightful fellow, isn't he?" Carol said as they drove back down the road.

"These backcountry people have a way of their own," Peter said. "Hey! There's the bridge!"

He drove over the new steel bridge. It was beautiful there with the brook and the different kinds of trees growing along it—and with Caleb Grimes out of sight.

"The storekeeper said *not* to cross the bridge, remember?" Carol said.

"Well," responded Peter confidently, "we must have circled around and come at it from the other side. Hey, there's the house!"

3

"Well, I see why that old guy in the store called it the bottle house," Adam said, as they got out of the car. "It sure is weird."

"That's exactly what it is," Carol said, "a bottle house. It was an experiment."

"A spearmint?" Becky asked. "Like gum?"

Her father laughed and said, "Ex-per-i-ment. It was made out of old bottles and other things people usually throw away. Look at those bottles by the front door." He pointed. "They make good insulation, and they also let in a beautiful light."

"I don't care what it's made of," Adam said. "But I thought it was gonna be big. I mean so Becky and me could have different rooms . . . for a change."

"Well," his mother said, "compared to our apartment, it's huge . . . well, bigger. It is a funny little house, though, isn't it?"

"Just right for our crazy little family," Peter said. "Hey, look at our backwoodsman, there." He pointed toward Adam who was climbing on some rocks in the brook.

"Adam, don't get—never mind—wet," Carol yelled as he slipped and fell into the water.

"Mom! Dad! This is great!" He brushed water and stringy blond hair out of his eyes. "There are fish here. Millions of 'em. Big ones, too! Dad, hey, can you get my rod?"

"No, it's getting late. You'll have to wait till tomorrow. Now, get out of there."

"Aw, Dad."

"Now!" Carol said. "You're going to catch cold."

Peter began untying the rope on the luggage rack, and Carol walked toward the front door. Becky ran up to her with a bunch of wild flowers.

"Here, Mumma. They're for our new house."

Carol hugged her and said, "Thank you, dear girl. I'm sorry that awful man frightened you."

"He was scary. I've never seen a wild fox before. Why did he want to kill it?"

"I don't know."

"Dad," Adam said, "please let me go fishing."

"Not now. Here, help me with this stuff." He handed Adam a suitcase and a duffel bag. "We've got to get unpacked before it gets dark. The fish will still be there tomorrow."

"Er, Peter," Carol said, "I hate to mention it, but where did the realtor say the key would be?"

"Let's see." He put his armload of luggage down. "Ah . . . Mr. Wicker said it would be hanging on a nail."

"Right, that's the way I remember it, too. Any particular nail, though?"

"Well, it has to be around here somewhere." He looked at her, helplessly. "Somewhere pretty obvious."

"Not too obvious, or why bother?"

"Boy, this is great," Adam said. "Some vacation house! First, we can't find it. Becky gets shot at. I can't fish, and now we can't even find the key!"

Carol looked around and behind the shutters, and Peter felt over the door. Adam tried a window, but it was locked.

"Here it is! Here, I found it!" Becky shouted. "Here, under the window."

"Good girl," her father said, taking the key from her. "That was thoughtful of them to put it at a child's eye level. We could have been out here all night."

"Well, the important thing is, Becky found it," Carol said.

"Wow! This is neat!" Adam said when they got inside.

The walls were rough white plaster, and the heavy rafters were hand-hewn and grayish-brown with age. The evening sun streamed in through the windows and bottles in the walls and gave the place a warm glow. The living room was small, but the high cathedral ceiling made it appear larger.

"Mumma, this looks just like a dollhouse—an old

one like when you were a little girl. Sasha and I are going to like it here."

Her mother smiled and said, "I think we're going to get along fine here."

Peter went out for the avocado tree and more luggage, and Adam started to follow, but then he saw something move on the fireplace mantel. "Hey, look, a mouse!"

"Where?" said Becky. "Let me see. Oh, look, isn't he cute!"

The little brown and white field mouse climbed up the chimney and scurried across a beam.

"I'm gonna catch it," Adam said, running across the room and jumping up on a chair. "He'll make a great pet."

"Not on your life," his mother said.

"Oh, why?" Adam moaned. "You afraid of a little mouse?"

"Er . . . no. I'm not afraid of a mouse, young man, but we're not going to keep one as a pet."

"What's this?" said Peter, coming through the door with the avocado tree.

"He's so cute," Becky said. "Can't we keep him? Don't hurt him, Adam."

"What's cute?" Peter asked, still holding the avocado.

"Look, Dad," said Adam, jumping to another chair. "It's a field mouse."

"I want that mouse out!" Carol yelled. "Out!"

Peter put the avocado down and said, "It is a cute little rascal, but . . ."

"Out! I said. I don't want a mouse living in our house."

"Aw, Mom," said Adam. "It's better than all the cockroaches in the city."

"Well," she said indignantly, "I don't like them either."

"Don't worry," Peter said. "There he goes." The mouse crawled through a crack between the wall and the chimney and disappeared. "Now, let's get the rest of our stuff. Becky, you get your dolls and animals, and take them upstairs. And Adam, you get some dry clothes on and help me."

Later, after dinner, Carol said, "I'm sorry about that mouse, kids, but I just didn't want it in the house. A field mouse belongs outside . . . in the fields."

Peter glanced at her and said to Becky and Adam, "You'll have lots of wild pets all summer. Now it's time for you two to get to bed. We've got a big day ahead of us tomorrow."

"Are we gonna get to go to one of those old iron furnaces you're writing about in your book?" Adam asked as he headed upstairs.

"Sure, but probably not tomorrow. We've got all summer."

Later, before she fell asleep, Becky whispered, "Good night, house, and good night, mouse, wherever you are."

4

The next morning, before anyone else was awake, Adam got dressed quietly and went out to the brook and began fishing. A couple of hours later Becky joined him, and he said, "This dough bait's no good. Will you do me a favor? Dig some worms for me? There's a shovel back by the garbage can."

"Sure." Becky found the shovel and began digging. After a few minutes, she shouted, "Adam! I got one, I found a worm!"

"Well, bring it here," said Adam, impatiently.

Becky watched the worm as it squirmed in her hand. Then she looked at Adam and said, "No! She's my pet, and her name is Alice."

Suddenly, Adam felt a tug on his line. "Becky, Becky,

look! I got one, I got one!" He reeled in the line and pulled out a large brown trout. "Wow, are we ever gonna have a good supper tonight!"

"Mumma, Popi!" Becky yelled. "Adam got a fish, a big fish, and I got a pet!" She ran into the house with Alice.

Later, after breakfast, Carol began digging a garden, and Peter set up his typewriter on a picnic table outside, near a quarry pond where Becky and Adam were swimming. After several dives with a mask and snorkel, Adam got out of the water.

"See anything?" his father asked.

"Naw, can't even see bottom. How deep you think this quarry is?"

"Pretty deep. It's an old limestone quarry. Not much life in it, I expect." He began typing again.

"There's lots of life along our brook, though," Adam said. "I saw all kinds of tracks. But how come we never see any animals?"

Peter stopped typing and said, "They must be nocturnal—creatures of the night." He got up. "Let's take a look at those tracks. Then maybe we can tell what they are."

"Hey, yeah. There's a book inside about wild life." Adam ran into the house and came back out with the book.

"Honey, you and Becky want to come with us? We're going to try to identify animal tracks along the brook."

Carol looked up and wiped perspiration from her brow. "No, you two go along. I've got to get the seeds in if we're going to have any vegetables before summer's over."

Adam and Peter walked upstream along the brook and into the woods. As they approached a clear pool, Adam said, "Hey, Dad, look at all the tracks here."

His father got down on his hands and knees and said, "It sure looks like somebody's favorite fishing place."

Adam looked through the book. Then he said, "I think most of these are raccoon tracks."

"I think you're right."

"Neato! Can I camp out here with a flashlight some night? I'd love to see 'em."

"If they're raccoons, we're going to have to watch our garbage," Peter said. "They're the best garbage raiders there are. Hey, why don't you rig up a trip wire that will turn on a light. That way, if they raid us tonight after supper—and they probably will—we can all see them."

"Yeah! That's a great idea."

All that afternoon Adam worked on the trip wire and light setup, and that evening after they had eaten, he left the lid off the garbage can, just to make certain the raccoons wouldn't pass them by. Once it was dark, he and Becky sat in their bedroom window and waited.

"We've been waiting here forever," Becky said. "I don't think . . ."

"Shhh. You'll scare 'em."

Becky left the window, and then a few minutes later a light flashed on over the garbage can.

"Hey, look, raccoons!"

Two raccoons stared at the light for a moment from inside the can, and then at the sound of Adam's voice, they scattered. One climbed up the back porch post to the roof, and the other, in his hurry to get away, tipped the can over and ran into the woods.

"Where?" Becky yelled, running outside with Adam. "Where are they?"

"The light scared them," Adam said, "but look! There's one on the roof." He shone a flashlight on the raccoon. "Isn't he beautiful?"

"Oh, yes."

Their parents came outside, and Peter said, "So you've got one, huh?"

"Yeah. Can we catch it, Dad? Raccoons make great pets."

"Oh, please," Becky begged.

"He's beautiful, all right," Carol said, "just the way he is, wild and free."

"Aw, Mom, what's wrong with having a pet?" Adam asked.

"I'll tell you one thing," Peter said. "The mess raccoons make isn't so beautiful. I wonder how country people keep raccoons out of the garbage?"

"I know," Adam said. "I bet they have a dog. Couldn't we get a dog? Please! This is the perfect place for a dog."

"That may be," his mother said, "but our apartment isn't. Our lease clearly says we can't keep *any* pets. The Baleekas would evict us just like that if we came home with a dog. So let's hear no more about it."

"Aw." Adam kicked at the garbage on the ground.

"Let's clean this mess up and go back inside," Peter said. "Tomorrow you and I can build a shed to keep these critters out of the garbage."

After they had put everything back into the can, the others went inside, but Adam stayed outside and watched the raccoon who was still on the porch roof. He picked up a crust of bread and climbed on top of the can. "Here, boy, here." He offered the bread to the raccoon.

Slowly, cautiously, the raccoon edged toward his hand. Then, just as he was about to take the offering, Carol came back outside and said, "Adam, what are you doing?"

Startled by her voice, Adam lost his balance and fell off the can, and the raccoon scurried away across the roof.

"Adam, are you all right?"

"Yeah, I'm okay, but darn it, you scared the raccoon away."

She helped him pick the can up, and as they went back inside, she said, "I'm sorry, Adam, I really am."

"I didn't want to cage it or anything. I just wanted us to be friends."

"I know, sweetheart. You want to be friends with all animals. It's a nice thought, but not easy to do. Wild animals have their own ways, you know. That's how they survive."

5

During the next several days the family settled into a summer routine. Peter and Adam built a shed that kept the raccoons out of the garbage *most* of the time. Carol worked hard in the garden, and by the end of the week, she had planted corn, radishes, cucumbers, summer squash, green onions, and a dozen tomato plants. Becky and Sasha had endless tea parties on the lawn near the picnic table where her father worked on his book. Usually in the afternoons when the sun was hottest, they would swim in the quarry pond. Adam caught trout almost every day and learned to clean and cook them himself.

Usually Adam got up before the others, and one morning, instead of fishing, he decided to explore farther upstream. The brook snaked up the gentle mountain slope. Birds sang happily from the trees, and squirrels and chipmunks chattered busily. Adam felt good. If only Dad's book makes a lot of money, he thought, we can move out of the city and maybe live here forever, and have a dog and cats, and maybe even a horse and a cow and a goat.

Whenever he came to a quiet pool in the brook, he saw all kinds of animal tracks—raccoons, skunks, deer, and others he couldn't identify, even with the book. Once he thought he recognized bear tracks. Higher up, near a large pool, he suddenly noticed different tracks. Dog tracks. They had to be. He looked around and saw they led into the woods and disappeared in the forest floor of humus, leaves, and pine needles. And then he saw another print—a man's large boot print. And then another and another. He followed the tracks farther upstream, and then he heard something. He stopped and listened. He heard it again. It was a whimpering sound.

Adam looked around and listened some more. Then he followed the weak sound into the woods. It got louder, and when he parted some mountain laurel, he looked down, surprised.

It was a dog. A long-haired, muddy mutt was lying in the mud, looking up at him and whimpering louder.

"Hey, boy, come here," Adam said, reaching for the dog. "It's okay. I won't hurt you."

Then he saw the blood, and then the trap on the dog's forepaw.

"Aw, fella, poor fella. How'd this happen?" Gently, he lifted the paw and trap and said, "It's gonna be okay now. I'll get you out of this thing."

The dog's nose was dry and warm as he nuzzled against Adam and licked his hand.

"Don't be afraid, boy. I'm gonna help you. I don't know who set this trap, but I'm your friend. I'll get you out of there."

The dog licked his hand again and looked at him helplessly. Adam put his arms around him and stared at the bloody paw. "Good boy, good boy," he said as he took the red bandanna from his forehead and slipped it over the dog's head. "Okay, fella, let's see if I can open this thing."

Adam inspected the trap, gently, and then he pulled on both sides of the steel jaws. "Easy, boy, easy. I know it hurts." He strained again, and finally he freed the bloody paw.

The dog sprang free, but then he fell back into the mud, yelping in pain.

"Easy, boy, easy. Here, let's wash this paw." Gently, he picked the dog up and carried him to a pool in the brook. He carefully washed the blood and mud off the paw, and the dog seemed to feel better. He rolled over and over in the cool water, and lapped it up. "Good boy, you feel better, don't you?"

While the dog continued to splash in the water, Adam went back to the trap. He released the chain that held it to a tree, and then he hung the trap on his belt. When he got back to the dog, he said, "We're gonna take this terrible thing with us!"

Adam picked the wet dog up and said, "Hey, you're white. Boy, a few minutes ago I didn't think so." Carrying the grateful dog, he began walking downstream.

When they got home, Carol looked up from the garden where she was hoeing. "What on earth!"

"It's a dog, Mom! He was caught in a trap, and he's hurt bad."

Becky ran up to them and said, "Where'd you find him? He's so cute. What's his name?"

"Becky, run and get your father," her mother said. "I think we'd better take this little guy to the veterinarian."

Adam held the dog on his lap on the way to the vet's office in town. The dog whimpered a little, but managed to wag his tail.

The vet was an older gray-haired man who didn't sound as though he had always lived in the country. Gently, he examined the dog's paw, and then he said, "No bones broken, but there's a lot of tissue damage. Poor fellow probably caused most of it himself, trying to get free. I've known dogs to chew a paw completely off to get out of a trap. They're nasty things, completely indiscriminate in what they catch. I see a lot of their unintended victims."

As the doctor bandaged the paw, Peter said, "You wouldn't have any idea whose dog it is, would you?"

The vet scratched the dog behind the ears and said, "I don't recognize him. He's probably just a summer dog. They come up with the summer people. A lot of them get left behind, or lost, or stray away. By the end of the summer, my kennel's full of strays. I try to find homes for them, but most of them have to be put away."

"That's terrible!" Carol said. "You mean some people just bring a dog along for their vacation, and then turn it loose?"

"I'm afraid so," said the vet as he handed the dog to Adam. "Of course, that might not be the case with this little hobo here. He's an attractive mutt. You might try advertising in the *Journal,* and see if you can locate the owner."

"That's a good idea," Peter said. "We'll try that."

As they left the vet's office, Carol said, "You've been very kind."

On the way home, Adam asked, "Do we have to put an ad in the paper? Can't we just keep him?"

Peter turned and glanced at his son. "Adam, you know the only fair thing is to advertise. If there's no answer in . . . say . . . two weeks from the time the paper comes out, well . . ."

"Well, what, Peter?" Carol asked. "You know the Baleekas would never let us keep him."

"Please, Mom," Adam said. "Maybe we could work out something with Mr. Baleeka about the lease."

"We have to!" Becky cried.

"I'll do all the walking and feeding and everything," Adam said.

Becky patted the dog and said, "You'd like to stay with us, wouldn't you, Hobo?"

Adam looked at her. "Where'd you get the name, 'Hobo'?"

"That's what the dog doctor called him, didn't he, Hobo?"

Hobo licked her on the face and wagged his tail.

"That's right, Becky," her father said, "but I think he meant . . . Well, it's a good name, though."

Carol looked around the car at all of them and finally said, "I smell a conspiracy here. You're going to give that dog a name, and he's going to worm his way into your little hearts. Then you'll never want to give him up."

"Already I don't want to give him up," Becky said. Tears were on her cheeks. "We can't give Hobo up."

"One by one," Peter said. "First, let's put the ad in the paper. Maybe the owners are right here in town. But while he's with us, we've got to call him something."

"I like Hobo," Adam said.

Becky wiped the tears from her eyes and said, "Me, too. Hi, Hobo. I hope your old family is far away and doesn't read newspapers."

That night when everyone else was asleep, Becky stared out the window by her bed and whispered, "Star light, star bright, first star I see tonight, wish I may, wish I might, grant this wish I wish tonight. Please, *please* don't let Hobo's old family see that ad!"

She lifted the covers and patted Hobo, who was sound asleep on her bed. Sasha had fallen, unnoticed, to the floor.

6

Every other day Adam and Becky changed Hobo's bandage, and his paw got better and better. He could run on three legs almost as well as most dogs can on four. Adam taught him how to sit and shake and speak, and Becky pretended she was a doctor who had been sent to the country to take care of this special patient.

One day when Hobo was just beginning to put some weight on his bandaged paw, Peter told Carol, "I found out about this old forge a few miles from here. They still make iron utensils by hand. I thought I'd take a look. You and the kids want to go?"

Carol looked up from a letter she'd been typing and said, "I'm sure the kids would. They should get away from Hobo for a few hours, just so they don't love him

43

to death. I'd love to go, too, but I've got a few letters to write. Do you know how many dolphins are killed every day just because they get caught in tuna nets? It's a crime, an unbelievable crime that these beautiful, free creatures are caught and killed by greedy, insensitive human beings. Oh, well . . . you and the kids go on. I've got some weeding to do, too, so I'd better stay. Hobo can keep me company."

Peter kissed her on the cheek and said, "Don't tell me he's beginning to worm his way into your little heart, too."

"Oh . . . well, darn it. Yes, he's a marvelous dog. Great for the kids in the country, but totally impractical for the apartment in the city."

"Okay, okay," said Peter as he opened the door to call Becky and Adam. "Don't overdo. We'll be home before suppertime."

"You always are." She laughed. "Have fun."

After she had written her letters, Carol went out to work in the garden. Hobo tagged along after her and *helped* with particularly stubborn weeds. "Hobo, old boy, you're a pretty good fellow," she said. Hobo licked her in the face and wagged his tail. But then suddenly he began to growl.

Carol looked up, and there, standing over her, was Caleb Grimes. He was still wearing the same filthy red and black shirt and carrying the rifle, as well as several traps. He laughed, a low, cold laugh, and his yellowed teeth gleamed in the bright sunlight. "I want my trap, lady," he growled.

"What is it? What do you want?" she demanded, standing up.

Hobo growled again as Caleb stepped closer.

"I've come for my trap," the big man said.

Carol stared him straight in the eyes and said, "I don't know what you're talking about."

"It's yer kid, lady. He stole my trap. I tracked him to the house."

Hobo circled around the trapper and began barking furiously.

"How very brave and clever of you to have tracked my son!" Carol said. "Adam didn't know it was yours. He just wanted to rescue this poor dog who was caught in it. Do you know, he nearly lost his paw!"

Caleb leaned on his rifle and said, "Lady, I want my trap!"

"Well, it's gone. None of us knew it was yours, so I told Adam to get rid of it. Why, one of my children could have gotten caught in that wretched thing and been maimed for life! I don't want to see you or your traps around here again, Mr. Grimes, or I'll call the sheriff!"

"Is that so? Well. I been trapping here on this place fer twenty years. I ain't gonna let no city folk stop me now!"

He stepped even closer, and Hobo gave him a low warning growl. Suddenly, Caleb swung the rifle butt and hit Hobo. "Git away, you mutt! Go on, git!" He swung again.

"Don't you touch that dog!" Carol shouted. "You've hurt him enough already. Hobo, come here. Come on, boy, we're going to call the sheriff." She grabbed his collar, the red bandanna, and said, "Don't bite him, boy. It would make you sick."

"Don't worry, lady," Caleb said. "I'm leavin'. But I don't take kindly to folks who steal other folks' property. Not kindly at all. You jest wait. I'll fix ya. I'll git even." He spit a wad of tobacco in Carol's direction and turned to leave. But then he turned back and said, "There's more than one way to skin a cat . . . or a dog, fer that matter!" With that, he laughed—an evil laugh—and turned again and walked away.

"Hobo, dear Hobo," Carol said, hugging the little dog.

Carol didn't see it, but when Caleb got away from the house, in the woods, he began setting more traps.

That evening, after Peter and the children got home from the forge, Carol waited until she could tell Peter in private about the visitor.

"I don't think he'll come back," Peter said, "but if he does, if he even pokes his ugly face out of those woods, there'll be no second thoughts about calling the sheriff."

A few days later Adam and Becky were able to take Hobo's bandage off for good. "There," said Adam, "you're almost good as new."

Hobo, to show off, ran around the meadow and then straight for the quarry pond, where he jumped and landed with a splash. Becky and Adam laughed and followed him into the pond.

Peter stopped typing and watched Hobo and the

kids as they splashed in the water. He was lost in thought when Carol ran up to him, shouting, "Peter, Peter, look! Our first harvest! Radishes! Aren't they beautiful!" She threw a bunch onto the picnic table.

"Wow! They sure are. Just like the book said. It took exactly four weeks." He wiped one off on his blue jeans and took a bite. "Hmmm, best I've ever had."

"It's kind of magical, isn't it?"

"It's a day to celebrate," Peter said as he got up from the bench. He picked Carol up and swirled her around. Then, more seriously, he said, "And you know what else it is?"

"No. What?"

"Well, the kids haven't said anything, but it's been exactly two weeks since our ad about Hobo appeared in the paper. I've got a feeling they've been counting."

Carol frowned. "What are we going to do? I mean I love Hobo as much as they do, but what are we going to do when we get back to the city?" She pointed toward Becky, Adam, and Hobo, who were still splashing in the pond. "Look at them. What are we going to do, Peter?"

Gently, he put his arm around her and said, "Well, I've been thinking. The Baleekas have a dog. Maybe we can work out something with Mr. Baleeka. A small increase in rent, for instance."

Carol pulled away. "I don't know what makes you think you can work something out with *that* man. There's nothing the Baleekas would like more than to evict us from our apartment. Once we're out of there, they can double—maybe even triple—what we're paying now."

Peter looked at her thoughtfully. "I know. But if we

can't keep him, surely we can find a home for him somewhere in the city. We can't just abandon him now and make him a true summer dog."

"I was afraid this would happen. But you're right. We can't leave him."

"Okay," said Peter, smiling, "let's celebrate this decision. We'll have a cookout in honor of the first radishes and Hobo."

"Aha, I knew your stomach would get into the act. Well, I just happen to have some hamburgers and hot dogs in the fridge."

"Great!" Peter ran to the pond and joined the kids and Hobo.

7

"Hey, Popi, look at Mr. Hobo!" Becky yelled. Hobo was wearing a straw hat and dancing around a tablecloth on the ground. Becky, Hobo, Sasha, and a doll were having a tea party.

Peter looked up from his typewriter on the picnic table and said, "Not now, Becky. I'm working."

"But Popi, look!" She turned to Hobo and said, "Mr. Hobo, how nice of you to come for tea. Do you take milk? I do—lots."

"Dad, Dad! You've got to help me with this teepee!" Adam yelled from the brook, where he was trying to set up several sapling poles.

"Rats!" Peter muttered as he crumpled up a piece

of paper. "Can't you kids see I'm trying to work? Summer's almost over, and I have to finish this darn book."

As he put a new sheet of paper in the typewriter, Carol called to him from the back porch. "I'm off to town to do the shopping and touch base with civilization. I haven't seen a paper in days."

"Okay, love," Peter said. "You'll find me right here when you get back. I'm afraid the words aren't flowing well this morning. Take the kids with you—please."

"Sorry, dear. I tried, but they said they're sick of town. They'd rather stay here. But I told them not to bother you."

"Right, just the way they haven't been."

"Don't worry. I'll talk to them again. Hope the words start flowing."

"Thanks. Me, too. Enjoy civilization. See you back here, mid-afternoon?"

"Thereabouts."

He began typing again.

Carol had been gone no more than fifteen or twenty minutes when Adam came up to his father. "Dad, you've got to help me with this teepee."

Peter yanked another sheet out of the typewriter and wadded it up. "Not now, Adam! Can't you see I'm trying to get some work done?"

Adam glanced at the several wads of paper around the table and said, "Well . . . okay. I guess I'll wait till you're finished."

"Can't you do something else?"

"Like what?"

"Like what! This isn't a rainy Sunday afternoon in the city. Take a walk, explore, fish, practice with the bow and arrow you made. Play with Hobo. Read! When did you last read a book?"

"Aw, Dad. I'm sick of doing those things. I want to build a teepee."

Peter sighed and said, "All right, what's the problem?" He got up and followed Adam to the brook.

"I just can't seem to get the frame up the way the Indians did," Adam said.

His father looked skeptically at the poles. "I don't know as much about Indian lore as you do, Adam. But I'm certain no self-respecting brave would try to make a teepee out of these poles. It's just logical. They have to be reasonably straight and about the same size."

"Aw, Dad, you mean start over?" He frowned and kicked at a stone.

"Well," said Peter, picking up a straight, long pole, "not entirely. Some of these are okay. If they were all like this one, you'd have no problem."

As they looked around for other long, straight saplings, Becky and Hobo ran up to them. "Popi, Hobo and I are hot. Can we go swimming in the pond?"

"No, Becky. You know the rule. Not by yourself." He glanced at Adam. "But wait a minute. Adam, why don't you go swimming with them?"

"Aw, Dad, I don't want to. Can't you see we're bored with the same old things, day after day?"

"Yeah," Becky said.

"Hey!" Adam said. "I've got an idea. Remember you

told us about an old iron furnace up the brook? You promised to take us there sometime. Couldn't we go today?"

"Yes, Popi, please. You promised!"

Their father shrugged and said, "Okay, okay. Maybe a change of scene will do us all good. But it's quite a hike up there. We'd better take some lunch. And let's not forget to leave a note for your mother, in case she gets back before we do."

"Sure, Dad," Adam said. "I'll make the lunch." He ran inside the house.

Becky clapped her hands and danced around Peter with Hobo. "Goody! Goody! We're going on an adventure. Come on, Hobo."

After Adam had fixed sandwiches and after Becky had changed from her tea-party dress to blue jeans, they began hiking along the brook. When they were a little over a mile from the house, Adam pointed and said, "This is where I found Hobo." Hobo sniffed around the tree where the trap had been chained and began to growl.

"Let's have lunch," Becky said.

"I don't think Hobo would like to hang around here," her father said. "Let's go a little higher. We still have a couple of miles, and there's no real trail."

They continued to hike, and after a while, Peter stopped and picked up a piece of slag. It was blue-green and looked like volcanic glass. "Well, we haven't passed it," he said. "As long as there's slag in the brook, we know we're downstream from the furnace."

"Can I see it, Dad?" Adam asked.

"Sure." He handed it to him. "This is the stuff that

was thrown away when they made iron in the furnace."

Becky picked up another piece and examined it. "It's pretty."

Peter looked around and said, "We're getting close. Why don't we eat here, here on this slag heap."

After they had eaten, and after Becky had collected more slag than she could possibly carry, Peter said, "Now that we have feasted on rare peanut butter and jelly sandwiches, let's explore this ancient work of man."

"Yeah, let's go," Adam said, running ahead of them. "Come on, Becky. Come on, Hobo!"

"Can I keep all of this slag, Popi?"

Her father laughed and said, "You can keep what you can carry. But leave it here for now. Nobody will take it. It's been here for a couple of hundred years already."

They walked on along the brook and through the woods until, finally, they came to the furnace.

"Wow!" Adam pointed. "Look at it. It looks like an old castle tower."

"Yeah, look, Hobo!" Becky squealed. "A real castle! Let's play king and queen."

The stone furnace was about twenty feet high, and it had been built into the side of a hill. At the base of the tower there was an opening that, Peter explained, had been for unloading the molten iron.

"Gee, this is neato," Adam said, looking around the opening.

"It was probably built around the time of the American Revolution," Peter said. "If we can get inside, I can tell from the maker's mark on the firebrick. If it hadn't been for this furnace and others like it, America might have lost the Revolution. Cannons from the iron made here were used to fight off the British."

Adam pulled a few rocks away from the opening and said, "Look, Dad, we can get in through here. Just have to move a few rocks, that's all."

Hobo went in first, and Becky and Adam crawled in after him. Peter had to get down on his belly to squeeze through, but he finally made it, too. "Be careful," he said, once they were inside the furnace. "This is an old falling-down ruin, and I don't want anybody hurt."

"Wow, look up there!" Adam said. "It sure is a long way to the top."

Peter looked up through the opening. "Yeah. In the old days they'd fill the furnace with iron ore and lime and charcoal, and get the whole thing going so hot that the mix would melt. Iron, being the heaviest, would sink, and they'd take the molten iron out here, where we came in. That slag you like so much, Becky, would float on top, and they'd dump it out by the brook where we had lunch."

Peter examined the inside of the furnace and said, "To keep the stone from melting, along with the iron ore, they lined the furnace with this firebrick."

As he spoke, Hobo looked up and began to growl.

"What is it? What's the matter, boy?" Adam asked. Then he looked up. "Oh!"

Peter, still examining the firebrick, said, "Hey, kids, look. Here's the maker's mark. Now we can tell when the furnace was made."

Hobo growled some more and then began barking furiously. Becky looked up and screamed.

"Ha! ha! ha!" came a deep voice from the rim of the tower.

"Grimes, what are you doing there?" yelled Peter, looking up, too, at the trapper who was still carrying his rifle and dangling traps over the rim.

"Makes a nice trap for city folk, don't it! Be careful now that loose stones don't block your entrance." He laughed again, and Peter and the kids could hear him knocking stones loose as he slid down the hill side of the furnace.

Suddenly there was a loud roar. Large boulders crashed down and blocked the opening they had used to enter the furnace.

"Popi! Popi!" Becky yelled. "We can't get out! Look!"

Peter ran to the entrance and pushed against the fallen rocks, but they wouldn't budge. "Grimes! Caleb Grimes! You've blocked the way. Help us! Caleb . . . please help us!" He tried again to push the rocks away, but he couldn't move them. He stepped back and looked up. "I guess there's only one way out, kids."

"We'll never be able to climb up there," Adam said. "It's too high and steep."

"Popi, Popi! I'm scared."

"Don't worry, honey." Peter hugged her. "We'll think of something. Adam, did you leave a note for Mom, telling her where we were going?"

Adam looked surprised. "No. I thought you were going to."

With a guilty expression, Peter said, "No, I guess I forgot."

"Oh, Popi, now we'll never get out."

"We'll get out, or someone will find us. Don't you worry."

As they looked around for handholds and footholds in the firebrick, Hobo began sniffing around the sealed opening.

"Hey, Dad!" Adam shouted. "Why don't we send a note to Mom with Hobo? I'll bet he can get through those chinks."

Peter looked at the sealed opening and said, "You're probably right. I suspect Hobo could get out. But what makes you think he'd take a note to Mom? He's a smart dog and all, but . . ."

"I think he would, that's all," Adam said. "I just think he would."

"Good boy. You'll go to Mumma, won't you?" Becky said, petting Hobo.

"Well," said their father, trying again to budge the rocks, "I guess we don't have much choice. It's worth a try."

As Peter wrote a note, Adam took a lace from one of his sneakers. He tied the note to the lace and then made a loop that he slipped over Hobo's head. "You can do it, boy. I know you can."

Becky hugged the dog and said, "You'll save us, won't you, Hobo?"

Adam pushed Hobo through a small chink between the fallen rocks and said, "Go home, boy." Hobo, once out, turned around and tried to get back in. "No, Hobo.

No! Go home! Take the note to Mom!" But Hobo kept trying to get back inside the furnace.

"It's no use, Dad. He wants to get back in with us."

"Be firm," Peter said. "Give him only one command."

Adam reached through the chink and pushed at Hobo. Firmly, he said, "Go home, Hobo! Go home!" But Hobo sat down and licked his hand. "Hobo! Go home! Aw, no!"

"Don't lose patience with him," Peter said. "He doesn't want to desert us."

Adam tried again. "It's okay, Hobo. Go home! That's a boy. Go home!"

Weakly, Hobo wagged his tail, and finally he turned away and trotted off into the woods.

"Good luck, Hobo!" Becky called.

Hobo ran along the brook, and then before he came to the tree where he had been caught in the trap, he cut off into the woods and headed on down the mountainside. Then, suddenly, he stopped and perked up his ears. He growled and then ran on.

Caleb Grimes saw the dog. He raised his rifle and shouted, "C'mere, ya little varmint!"

Hobo disappeared in the thick woods, and Caleb chased after him, yelling all the time. Hobo paused, and just as Caleb was about to aim his rifle, the dog reversed his direction and ran right past the trapper. Caleb turned so quickly that he lost his balance and fell into a bramble bush.

"Ow! Ow! Ow!" yelped Caleb. "You'll pay fer that one!" He chased after Hobo again, and just as he was about to catch up with him, Hobo came to the brook and leaped over it. Caleb tripped again, and this time he fell right in the middle of a pool. "Okay, yer in fer it now!" he yelled, shaking water off himself.

Caleb ran along the brook and then came to a meadow where he saw Hobo running toward a stone wall. "Now I gotcha, ya little varmint!" He raised his rifle, and just as he fired, Hobo leaped over the wall, but instead of running into the open meadow, he ran along the wall.

Caleb got to the wall and looked around, but he couldn't see Hobo. Then he climbed over the wall and saw the dog running alongside it. "Okay, I gotcha this time." But, as he took aim, Hobo disappeared in the woods at the end of the wall.

"Darn!" grumbled Caleb, dropping his rifle to the ground.

Hobo circled around Caleb in the woods and ran back to the brook that led to the house. When he got there, Carol was looking around, calling for Peter and the kids. Then she saw Hobo running toward her.

"Hobo! Thank heavens! Where have you been? Peter, Adam, Becky! Where are you?"

Hobo whined and paced back and forth, and finally Carol saw the note. Quickly, she read it and said, "Hobo, take me to Peter. Take me back. Take me to Peter and Adam and Becky."

Hobo ran toward the brook, and Carol followed.

When they finally got to the furnace, Hobo squeezed back in through the chink in the rocks.

"Hobo!" yelled Adam. "You did it!"

"Good boy, good boy!" Peter said, patting Hobo.

From outside the furnace, Carol shouted, "Peter! Adam! Becky!"

"Mumma, Mumma!" Becky danced around with Hobo. "You found us!"

"Carol," said Peter, peering through the chink, "find a long branch, anything, and try to pry these rocks away. That big one."

From the inside Peter and Adam pushed as Carol pried from the outside. Finally, the largest boulder gave way, and they were able to move the others with their hands. As soon as the opening was big enough, Becky and Adam edged through. They moved a few more rocks, and Peter squeezed through, too.

Once they were all outside the furnace, Carol said, "I was so worried. What happened? How did you get trapped?"

"Well," Peter said, brushing dirt from his clothes, "I was trying to find a maker's mark on the firebrick when . . ."

"Caleb Grimes did it!" Adam interrupted.

"Yeah!" said Becky. "He tried to bury us!"

"Caleb Grimes!" Carol wrung her hands. "He ought to be . . ."

"Wait!" Peter said. "One at a time. Caleb was on the rim of the furnace above us, and when he . . ."

Adam interrupted again. "He said it was a trap for city people!"

"Hold on, Adam," Peter said. "Yes, Caleb did say

that . . . and when he ran down the side of the furnace, he started the rock slide that trapped us in here."

"And he didn't even try to help you?" Carol asked. "What a hateful man!"

"He's not my favorite person in the world, either," said Peter, "but I don't honestly believe he intended to trap us. It all happened so fast. I think it was just bad luck."

Carol hugged Adam and Becky. Then she said, "I think we should call the police. That man is dangerous."

8

A few days after the iron furnace incident, the family and Hobo were sitting around a camp fire, cooking hot dogs and roasting freshly picked corn from the garden. It was a warm August evening, and the sounds of katydids and crickets filled the air.

"You know," Peter said to Carol, "I first thought a garden was a foolish idea."

She looked at him suspiciously.

"Not only because of our lack of experience, but also because we got started so late in the season. But I have to admit that this is the sweetest, freshest corn I've ever tasted."

"Yeah," agreed Adam. "Can't I have more corn instead of these yukky green beans?"

"Yukky! And after all my hard work," Carol grumbled. "You've got to have greens. They're loaded with vitamins. By the way, while we're enjoying all these good things from the garden, there are others who seem to appreciate it, too."

"Huh, what do you mean?" asked Peter, still munching on corn.

"Something's been eating the garden besides us."

Peter laughed. "Probably those raccoons again, getting even for the garbage shed we made."

"Maybe, but I don't think so," Carol said. "How would they get corn that's at least four feet from the ground?"

"Corn! What's getting our corn?" Adam asked.

"I don't know. Just something," his mother said.

"I bet it's deer." Adam looked out toward the garden. "I've seen their tracks around. Hey, I know! I'll set a sapling snare, like the Indians did. It really works."

"A what?" Carol asked. "What's a sapling snare?"

"I'll show you. We've got some rope, haven't we, Dad?"

"Sure, but do you really think you can rig one up?"

" 'Course I can."

After they had eaten, they took a rope from the shed, and Adam climbed up a tall sapling and tied an end of the rope near the top, while Peter pounded a trigger stake into the ground. Then they all pulled on the rope and bent the sapling to the ground. Adam looped the rope around the stake and said, "See, this holds the tree down."

He covered the stake with some brush. "Now, this should catch our corn thief by its leg."

"Won't it hurt the deer?" Becky asked.

"Naw. It'll just lift his leg up and probably teach him a lesson."

Peter examined the snare skeptically and said, "Why don't you rig up a trip wire to our flash camera, just in case your snare misses? At least we'll have a picture of the culprit."

"Hey, that's a great idea!" Adam said. "We'd better hurry, though, before it gets too dark."

Later that night, while Peter and Carol were reading in the living room, Adam sat in the dark kitchen and stared out toward the garden. Becky and Hobo had fallen asleep on the sofa.

"Adam," Carol said, "better hit the hay."

"Aw, Mom, can't I stay up just a little longer?"

"Absolutely not." She came into the kitchen. "It's way past your bedtime as it is." She yawned. "In fact, it's about our bedtime, too."

Peter came into the kitchen and patted Adam on the head. "Who knows," he said, "that deer, or whatever, may be a five A.M. raider. Or he may not come at all. There's no guarantee we'll catch the thief, you know. But I promise, if there's any action out there, I'll wake you up. Okay?"

"Oh, okay," Adam said as he headed toward the stairs. "Good night."

Carol turned off the last lights as Peter lifted Becky off the sofa.

Adam sat in the dark on the end of his bed and stared out into the darkness. Then, suddenly, there was a flash of light and a loud cry from the garden.

"Mom! Dad!" He grabbed a flashlight from his bureau and ran downstairs. "We caught something!"

"I know," Peter said, following him downstairs.

Becky woke up, and she and Carol and Hobo hurried down the stairs, too.

"Help! Somebody help!" came an angry voice from the garden.

Hobo ran ahead and began growling.

"Look!" said Adam when they got outside. "It's Caleb Grimes."

Caleb was hanging upside down by one leg and flailing his arms as Hobo barked at him.

"Be quiet, Hobo," Peter said.

"Well, well," said Carol as Adam held the light in Caleb's face, "the trapper gets trapped. That's poetic justice for you. But what were you doing, stealing our vegetables?"

Caleb twisted on the rope and tried to reach the loop around his ankle, but it was no use. His rough, booming voice had been reduced to miserable, low moans. Almost —but not quite—apologetically, he said, "I always take from summer people. It's my way of gettin' even." He tried again to reach the rope. "I took from you 'cause yer vegetables were the best. And besides"—he growled this time—"yer girl ruined my shot, and yer boy stole my trap. Now, let me down!"

Peter took the flashlight from Adam and held it in

"City folk! Ha! Why do you folks come up here where you don't belong?"

Adam carried the wounded Hobo home.

Adam and Kenneth try to unravel the mystery surrounding the Baleekas.

"Hobo, from here on in, you and me are going to be together."

"We got a good thing going. Don't mess it up!"

Adam and Becky spy on Mr. Baleeka in the cellar.

Adam and Hobo watch Mrs. Baleeka as she meets
with a strange man in the park

"Mr. Hobo, how nice of you to come for tea."

Hobo relaxes with a football after a game with Adam and Becky.

Caleb Grimes returns for his trap.

Caleb's face. "I'll let you down in a minute. But first . . . did you know you sealed us in that furnace the other day?"

"I didn't mean no harm. I jest wanted ta scare ya."

"Okay, I'll accept that, though we were tempted to call the police. But I want you to know that the flash that went off took your picture. If you come around here one more time, I'm going to have it printed in the newspaper. Then everybody in town will see how city folk made a fool out of Caleb Grimes."

"Yeah, yeah. Now, lemme down. I promise I won't come here no more."

Peter pulled on the rope until Caleb's hands reached the ground, and Adam slipped the loop over his foot. Caleb sat against a tree and brushed his clothes off.

"You say you take from gardens to get even," Carol said. "But do you ever take food because you're hungry, too?"

"Aw," said Caleb, embarrassed, "well, I never was no good at growin' things."

"Here," she said, putting squash and corn in his lap, "take these. But I don't want to see you around this place again."

Caleb got up slowly. Anxiously, he said, "Don't worry, ma'am. I'll not be back." Clutching the squash and corn, he limped off into the darkness.

"Strange character, isn't he?" Peter said as they walked back toward the house.

"And you know," Carol said, "he's hated us from the moment we came here, without even knowing us. It's a terrible thing, hatred. It does things to you. Warps you, somehow."

"That snare worked beautifully, didn't it?" Adam said. "Those Indians sure knew their stuff."

"Yeah," said Becky.

9

The family had one last picnic near the old iron furnace. Becky, Adam, and Hobo were playing inside the furnace, which only a week and a half earlier had been their prison. Carol and Peter were sitting on a large flat rock in the sun.

"I can't really believe we'll be back in the city in two days," Carol said.

Peter stretched and said, "Between Hobo and Caleb Grimes, it's been some summer."

"The good and the bad." Carol leaned forward. "Peter, what are we going to do about Hobo when we get back?"

"Don't worry. We'll work something out with Baleeka."

"Really, Peter, you keep saying that, but what if we can't?"

As she said it, Hobo scrambled out from the iron furnace, and Becky and Adam came out after him.

"Dad, Mom, can we go pick huckleberries?" Adam asked. "There's a place down the trail a ways that's loaded with 'em."

"Sure," Carol said. "Just be careful."

With Hobo in the lead, Becky and Adam ran toward the trail. "Don't go far. We want to leave pretty soon," Peter called after them.

"Okay," Adam shouted.

After they had gone, Carol, who was lying on the rock with her head on Peter's chest, said, "Do you think Caleb Grimes is a really bad person, or just somebody who can't cope with today's world?"

"Huh?" Peter said absently. "I don't know. Do you think Baleeka is a bad person? He sure copes with today's world."

Sitting up, Carol said, "I think he's sinister. There's something devious about him."

"Yeah. I've never been able to figure how he can make as much money as his wife spends. It can't all come from that wreck of a building we live in."

"He never spends a nickel on it, that's how. And he gets old tenants like us out so he can double the rent. I just know he'll never let us keep Hobo. And, despite the Baleekas, I love that place. I don't want to move."

Sighing, Peter said, "We can't afford to move, not unless my book becomes a best-seller, and that's not likely."

"So, what do we do about Hobo?"

Peter stood up and stretched again. "It's so nice here. Just take in a deep breath of that . . ."

"Peter, I'm sorry, but sometimes I don't think you appreciate the problem that dog is going to be." Carol stood up, too.

"Speaking of that rascal," Peter said, looking off to one side where Hobo and Adam were coming up the trail.

"Boy," said Adam when he got to the rock, "are those huckleberries good." He glanced around. "Hey, where's Becky?"

"What do you mean?" his mother asked in an alarmed tone of voice.

"She was with you!" Peter said.

"But she got tired and came back . . . didn't she, boy?"

Hobo looked up at Adam and wagged his tail.

"She did *not* come back!" Peter said, jumping down from the rock. "Becky! Becky!" he called.

"Where could she be?" Carol climbed down from the rock, too. "Becky! Becky! Where are you?"

"She can't be far," Adam said.

"Then why doesn't she answer?" snapped Peter. "Becky! Becky!"

"Dad, you know she never listens."

Carol, looking worried, said, "Adam, this is serious! She could be lost up here."

Peter walked toward the trail Becky and Adam had first followed. "There are so many trails around here. It's pretty confusing."

"Maybe we should all take different trails," Carol suggested.

"We might *all* get lost that way," Peter said. "We'd better stick together."

Carol looked helplessly at Peter and then at Adam. "Dear God, I hope she hasn't fallen. She could be hurt. Oh, no! Doesn't Caleb Grimes live up here some place!"

"Carol," Peter said nervously, "let's not panic. Caleb promised he wouldn't bother us anymore."

"Down by the house, yes, But we're in *his* territory now. Peter, I'm scared."

"Don't worry, Mom," Adam said. "She can't be far. She only left a little while ago. Hobo can find her, can't you, boy? Where's Becky? Go find her."

Hobo wagged his tail and began sniffing the ground. Then he began running down the trail.

"That a boy!" Adam yelled. "Go find Becky!" He turned toward his parents and said, "Come on. Let's go!"

They followed Hobo down the trail. He stopped, sniffed, and then turned off on another path. "Good Hobo, good boy," Adam said. "This must be the way she went."

They chased after him and stopped when he did. Hobo sniffed and then growled at something covered by a pile of leaves.

"What is it, boy?" said Adam. "What's the matter?"

"Wait!" Peter shouted. He picked up a stick and poked at the leaves. Suddenly there was a loud CLACK, and Peter jerked the stick back. A trap had snapped shut on it. "This is Caleb Grimes territory, all right."

"Oh, Peter!" said Carol, trying not to cry.

"It's all right, Hobo," Adam said. "Where's Becky? Go find Becky!"

Hobo led them on down the trail. Then he suddenly turned and headed toward a huge boulder. He stopped and looked back at the others from the top of the rock and began barking. Then he looked the other way and wagged his tail.

"Hey, Mom, Dad, there's a waterfall up there!" Adam yelled. "Hear it?"

They ran up to Hobo, who was still barking and wagging his tail. "Well, I'll be," Peter said.

Caleb Grimes and Becky were sitting on a rock ledge over a pool and fishing together.

"That darned dog!" shouted Caleb. "Git him outta here!" He raised his arm.

Peter and Carol ran to Becky and hugged her. "My baby!" Carol said. "You're all right!"

Becky looked up calmly and said. " 'Course I'm all right. Mr. Grimes has been teaching me how to catch trout." She turned to Hobo and scolded him. "And you, you bad dog, made us lose our fish!"

"Oh, come on," Adam said. "He was only trying to find *you.*"

"You see, honey," Peter said, "we didn't know where you were."

Adam shrugged and said, "See, I told you she'd be okay."

"Yeah," grumbled Caleb. "Well, she might not a been okay if I hadn't looked after her. Even city folk should know better than to let little kids go wanderin' off alone on the mountain."

71

Peter glanced at Carol. Then he said, "You're right, Mr. Grimes. We owe you our gratitude."

"Caleb Grimes, you're absolutely right!" Carol said warmly. "And I thank you. We all thank you." She grabbed his hand.

Embarrassed, Caleb quickly shook her hand. Then he got up and packed his gear. "Yeah, well, I gotta git." He paused for a moment and gave Becky a gentle pat on the head. "Maybe we'll meet again someday."

"I sure hope so, Mr. Grimes," Becky said as Caleb disappeared into the brush.

"Well, young lady," Carol said after Caleb had gone, "don't you go wandering off again. You had us all worried to death."

"I won't, Mumma."

Hobo led the way back to the flat rock near the iron furnace where they had left the picnic basket. As they followed the trail along the brook, Peter said, "You've saved us again, Hobo."

"Oh, Dad," said Adam, "can't we stay just a few days longer?"

"I wish we could, but I've got to be back Tuesday and get my work to the publisher. And the next day, my friend, you have school. It's hard to believe, but the day after tomorrow we'll be back in the city."

10

The city looked dull and drab when the Normans got back late Monday afternoon. The air was hot and still, and it smelled foul compared to that in the country. Peter double-parked in front of the apartment building and said, "Okay, gang, let's get this stuff out. Adam, you take Hobo for a quick walk. And don't forget the leash. We're in the city again."

He got out of the car and opened the hatchback for Becky, Adam, and Hobo. Then he went to the other side of the car and opened the door for Carol and the avocado tree, which had gotten much larger during the summer.

A horn honked. "Hey! Move it, mister!" shouted a taxi driver as Peter took the tree from Carol. "You're blocking traffic!"

Adam clipped the leash to Hobo's new collar, which had replaced the red bandanna, and said, "Well, this is the city, boy."

Hobo sniffed around and barked happily.

As Adam and Hobo started down the street, Mrs. Baleeka and Gigi met them. Mrs. Baleeka was wearing a bright pink, silky dress and a matching hat and gloves, and Gigi, who looked as though she had just come from the poodle parlor, was wearing a pink ribbon. The dogs greeted each other happily, and their tails were wagging.

"Hi, Mrs. Baleeka," Adam said. "How do you like our dog?"

Mrs. Baleeka glared at Hobo and said, "Where did you find that horrid little mutt?"

Proudly, Adam said, "In a raccoon trap. I rescued him!"

"Well!" said Mrs. Baleeka, scooping Gigi up in her arms, "whatever it is, you can't keep it. Ask your mother—your lease says 'no pets'."

Carol, holding the avocado tree, walked over to them and said, "I know about the lease, Mrs. Baleeka. But Hobo's such a good dog, so quiet and well behaved, that we hoped you and Mr. Baleeka would make an exception. Just this once."

Hobo began dancing at the end of his leash and barking loudly, trying to get back to Gigi. Mrs. Baleeka backed up and clutched Gigi, who was straining to jump away from her.

"No, Hobo! No!" yelled Carol. "Adam, you've got to control him."

Adam tugged at the leash, and as he did, Gigi jumped

from Mrs. Baleeka's grasp and began playing with Hobo.

"Gigi, precious!" shrieked Mrs. Baleeka. "Get that horrid beast away!"

Adam untangled the two leashes and said, "Come on, Hobo."

Peter, carrying a cardboard box, ran to them and said, "Here, Mrs. Baleeka, let me help." Then he dropped the box, and summer treasures—Becky's slag, dried flowers, a bird's nest, and several other things—spilled out all over the sidewalk.

As Peter tried to apologize, Bill, the apartment superintendent, came out of the building. He was tall and dark and tough-looking, and while he didn't have a beard, he made Adam think then of Caleb Grimes. He looked even meaner, though.

Bill grabbed Gigi and said, "Here ya go, Miz Baleeka."

"Oh, thank you, Bill," said Mrs. Baleeka. She cuddled Gigi, and then she turned to the Normans and squealed, "If you try to keep that horrid beast, you'll be breaking your lease, and we'll evict you!" Then she pranced into the building with Bill and Gigi.

As Peter and Carol picked up the things that had spilled, Carol said, "Welcome home."

The next afternoon Peter went down to the Baleekas' apartment and knocked.

"Yeah," yelled Mr. Baleeka from inside. "Who is it?"

"Ah, er . . . it's Peter Norman, Mr. Baleeka. I've got the September rent check."

Mr. Baleeka opened the door. He was wearing blue,

pinstriped trousers and a sleeveless white undershirt. His stomach hung out over his belt. "I'll take yer check, Norman, but I won't cash it. Till you get rid of that dog, you're breaking your lease."

"Sure, I understand that," Peter said. "But I thought maybe we could talk. I'd be willing to pay a little more each month to keep the dog."

Mr. Baleeka scratched his balding head and said, "I can't change the lease . . . but I'll tell you what, Norman. I can give you a new one. You've been in that apartment over twelve years. Today I could get more 'an twice what you're paying. You want to pay double, I'll do you a favor. I'll get you a new lease."

"I can't afford to double my rent," Peter said. "Be reasonable, Mr. Baleeka. I'm willing to pay fifteen or even twenty dollars a month more to keep the dog."

Mr. Baleeka grinned and said, "It's been nice having you for a tenant, Norman. In sixty days I evict. And now, I got business to attend to." He shut the door in Peter's face.

As the door slammed, Adam and Hobo came down the stairs. "Hi, Dad. Hobo and I are just on our way out. What business does Mr. Baleeka have, anyway?"

"Huh?" mumbled Peter, looking up. "Oh, I don't know. The old Scrooge certainly doesn't spend much time or money on this building."

"I was just wondering. See ya." He and Hobo walked toward the door.

"Yeah," Peter said. "Have fun in the park, but be careful. Remember, Hobo's a country dog."

Hobo and Adam ran in the park, they climbed over rocks, chased pigeons and squirrels, and Adam threw sticks for Hobo to retrieve. Twice Hobo jumped into the boat pond, and the second time he brought out an old sneaker.

"Good boy, Hobo," Adam said, jumping back as Hobo shook the water off. "But let's leave this old shoe here." Hobo dropped the sneaker and wagged his tail. "Oh, Hobo, you're the best dog in the whole world. I love you more than anything." He hugged the wet dog, and Hobo licked his face. "Well, guess we better get back home. We gotta eat, and I gotta get ready for school tomorrow."

They walked along the top of a high stone wall. Below them people were sitting on park benches. As they got close to the end of the wall, near the park entrance, Adam stopped short and whispered, "Look, Hobo. Down there. It's Gigi and Mrs. Baleeka."

Hobo wagged his tail and pulled at the leash. "Shhh. Let's spy on 'em." They crouched down on the wall and watched.

Mrs. Baleeka was still wearing the same silly pink dress, hat, and gloves, and she was holding a matching pink parasol. Gigi was wearing the pink ribbon, and even though it was warm outside, she was wearing a dog coat.

A short, tough-looking man with wire rim glasses, and wearing bright green trousers and a wrinkled white shirt, sat down next to Mrs. Baleeka and Gigi. He patted the poodle on the head, and as he did it, Mrs. Baleeka looked straight ahead and anxiously tapped her foot on the pavement. Then the man quickly slipped something under Gigi's coat and got up and left.

"That's strange," Adam whispered to Hobo. "Very strange. Let's hurry home and tell Becky." They jumped off the wall and ran all the way back to the apartment building.

When they got back, Carol was in the kitchen cooking. Peter wasn't home. Becky listened quietly as Adam told her about Mrs. Baleeka and the suspicious-looking man. "Really?" she said after he had finished.

"I swear it. The man slipped something under Gigi's coat. There's something fishy going on around here, and we've got to find out what it is. If we can just get something on the Baleekas . . ."

Becky's eyes widened. "You mean we'll be detectives?"

"Right. From now on, the Baleekas are under our surveillance."

"Huh?" Becky said, frowning. "What's that mean?"

"It means we watch 'em."

"Aw, is that all?" She sighed.

"I mean we *spy* on 'em."

"Oh, goody!" She clapped her hands.

11

Every day after school for the next few weeks Adam and Becky took Hobo to play in the park. They kept an eye on Mrs. Baleeka, but nothing suspicious happened. And then late one day in early October when Becky was staring out at the street through the apartment window, she suddenly yelled, "Adam! Adam, look! Mrs. Baleeka is taking Gigi to the park."

Adam ran to the window and watched for a moment. Then he said, "Yeah, and look, Gigi's wearing that stupid little coat again, and she has a ribbon, too—a blue one this time. Great, let's go. Come on, Hobo, let's go to the park."

"Wait a minute," their mother said as they started out the door. "Just where do you two think you're going?"

"Er . . . to the park," Adam said.

She eyed them suspiciously. "But you just got back from there. Now, what's going on?"

"Nothing, Mumma," Becky answered. "It's Hobo. I think he *has* to go out."

"Oh, okay, but don't stay long. We're having an early supper."

"We won't," they both said, slamming the door behind them.

As they hurried down the four flights of stairs, Adam said, "Now, do like I told you. Tag along, and when you have a chance, play with Gigi. Try to find out if there's a pocket in her coat."

When they got to the street, they ran and took a shortcut to the park. Adam and Hobo hid behind some bushes, and Becky pretended she was playing hopscotch on the sidewalk. When Gigi and Mrs. Baleeka got close, Becky suddenly fell to her knees and began hugging the poodle. "Oh, Gigi. I love you, more than any doggie, 'cept Hobo, of course."

Taken by surprise, Mrs. Baleeka shouted, "What are you doing? You let go of Gigi, you brat." She yanked on the little dog's leash, and Becky let go.

Mrs. Baleeka stood over Becky and said, "You have that mutt of yours to hug and pet." She laughed nastily and added, "Not for long, though, unless you want to be evicted."

"C'mon, Becky," Adam said, stepping from behind the bushes and taking her hand. "Let's go play." Hobo and Gigi wagged tails at each other.

Adam, Becky, and Hobo ran behind the stone wall, and then peered over it. Mrs. Baleeka sat on the same bench where Adam had seen them before.

"Look," Adam whispered. "Here he comes." He pointed to the suspicious-looking man who approached the bench. "It's the same man. See! Watch!"

"Yeah," said Becky.

"Shhh."

The man glanced at Mrs. Baleeka and Gigi, but then he walked on by.

"I don't understand," Adam said as they headed back toward the apartment. "It doesn't make sense. That *is* the same man who put something under Gigi's coat last time."

After Adam and Becky had gone to bed that night, Carol and Peter talked about their problem—Hobo.

"Twenty-eight phone calls to friends, and friends of friends," Carol said, "and not one of them wants a beautiful, intelligent, loving dog. Not even for free."

Holding a newspaper, Peter said, "Neither did you once. Remember?"

Carol sank down in the sofa next to him and sighed. "I know, but now that I've come to love that funny-looking mutt, we can't keep him. It's just too cruel—especially to the kids, and Hobo."

"I know." He put his arm around her. "I've been looking at apartments for rent," he said, waving the paper, "but there's nothing in this part of town—nothing we can afford."

"Peter, I could have told you that. You're a nice guy and everything, but your head's up there in the clouds somewhere."

Peter glanced at Hobo, who was sleeping on the floor, and said, "Why don't we advertise in the paper? There must be somebody in this city who'd like Hobo for a pet."

"It's worth a try," Carol said, sadly. "But we have to check out any prospective takers. Hobo doesn't get given to just anybody. Right, Hobo?"

Hobo looked up and wagged his tail.

That Saturday, when Becky and Adam were dumping garbage into the big cans in the basement, Adam whispered, "You hear something?"

Becky listened and said, "No."

"Quiet. I heard something. Listen. Here, behind that padlocked door." He put his ear against the door. "Yeah. Someone's talking in there."

Becky put her ear against the door, too. "Yeah. Look through the keyhole."

"That's just what I was gonna do." He stooped down and squinted through the hole beneath the padlock. Then he turned to Becky and said, "It's Mr. Baleeka. He's wearing that gun again, and he's paying Bill a lot of money."

The talk behind the door stopped, and they heard footsteps. Adam grabbed Becky's hand, and they hid behind a pile of trunks and wooden crates on the other side of the dimly lit basement.

They stared at the door, and Becky whispered,

"How'd they get in? The door's locked from the outside."

"Hey, you're right! That means somebody has to come and let them out." He frowned. "That's screwy."

"I'm scared," Becky said. "Let's go." She stood up.

"No, wait," Adam said, pulling her back down behind the crates and trunks. "I want to see who comes to let 'em out." He looked over the top of the pile. Then he put his finger to his lips. "Shhh."

From behind the door, they heard Mr. Baleeka say, "This is a big one, Bill."

Then the door opened, and Becky and Adam realized the padlocked hasp was a dummy. Mr. Baleeka slipped a jacket on and concealed the shoulder holster. As he and the superintendent walked toward the elevator, he said, "I want no mistakes. Got that, Bill?"

Bill shrugged and said, "Don't worry, Joe. You worry too much."

When the two men got in the elevator, Adam stood up and said, "Did you see that? A dummy lock. Let's go see what's in that room."

"No. I'm scared," Becky said. "Let's go."

"There's nothing to be afraid of," Adam said, leading her toward the door. "This may be our only chance."

When they got to the door, Adam tried it, but this time it was really locked. "Rats!" he said. "He must have locked it here." He pointed at the keyhole. Then he bent down and looked through it. "Darn! The light's off, too."

"Good," Becky said. "Let's get out of here."

"Good!" Adam said. "What do you mean, 'good'? We've got to find out what they're up to!"

Becky stared anxiously at the elevator door and said,

"Let's tell Mumma and Popi and let them find out."

"Are you kidding!" He glared at his sister. "If they knew we were spying on the Baleekas, they'd be furious, and make us stop. Look, Becky, if we don't get something on them and do it quick, we're gonna lose Hobo. You can quit trying if you want to. I'd understand. It is a little scary. But don't you see, if we can get something on Mr. Baleeka that he doesn't want people to know, then maybe we can make a deal with him, and he'll have to let us keep Hobo. Understand?"

Becky shrugged and said, "I guess so."

She started toward the elevator, but Adam stopped her and said, "Whether you quit or stay, you have to promise not to tell anyone about it. Okay?"

"Okay, I promise." When they got in the elevator, she said, "And I'll stay, too."

Adam put his arm around her and said, "Good."

That night, as they were getting ready for bed, Adam said, "You know, Mom's always talking about how animals need freedom. Remember that field mouse and the raccoon we tried to catch when we first got to the country?"

"Uh-huh," Becky said.

"Well, Mom was right. They were wild animals, but Hobo's different. All dogs are. He needs us, just the same way Mom and Dad need each other."

"Yeah, and we need him, too," Becky said, hugging Hobo, who was on her bed. "He's freer living with us than he would be caught in some trap."

"We're the ones who aren't free," Adam said. "We

always gotta do what grown-ups say. Even Mom and Dad aren't free. Just because Mr. Baleeka says we can't have pets, they . . ."

"Phooey!" Becky interrupted. "No one gets to be free—specially grown-ups and dogs like Hobo."

12

As November grew near, Carol and Peter still hadn't found a home for Hobo. A few people answered the ad in the paper, but no one wanted a middle-aged, middle-sized mutt. They wanted either an adorable little puppy or a great big guard dog. Hobo didn't fit either category. Peter had tried talking with Mr. Baleeka again, but the landlord wouldn't listen. "The mutt goes by the sixth, or you do," Mr. Baleeka had said.

Finally, on the Saturday before Halloween, a woman named Buel called and said she was interested in a free dog for her six-year-old daughter. Carol described Hobo, and Mrs. Buel said she and her husband and daughter would come by in an hour or so.

"Well," said Carol after she finished talking with Mrs. Buel, "I think we've solved one problem, but how do we tell the kids?"

"It's going to be tough," Peter said. "But we don't have a choice. I guess now's the time to do it. Where are they?"

"In the cellar," Carol said. "Dumping the garbage. It's strange, but I haven't had to ask them to take it down even once these past several weeks."

"They're growing up," Peter said.

When Adam and Becky returned from the basement, Becky ran over to Hobo who was asleep on the floor by Carol's desk, and Adam said, "I'll be right back. Have to get his leash."

"Adam . . . wait a minute," his father said, nervously. "In just a few minutes a family is coming over to see if they want to adopt Hobo."

"No!" Becky screamed, clutching Hobo in her arms.

"Becky, Adam," Carol began. "I . . . I know how much it hurts. I love Hobo, too. But we simply can't keep him in this apartment, and we can't find any other apartment that we can afford."

"We want to find the very best home we can for Hobo," Peter said.

"This is the best home for Hobo!" Becky said, crying.

"Hobo doesn't hurt the apartment or anything," Adam said. "I don't understand what the thing is about the lease." He struggled to keep from crying, too.

Peter glanced at Carol, and then he said, "It's simply

the legal agreement you make when you rent a place. Many, like ours, say you can't keep pets."

"That's stupid!" Adam shouted.

Later, as they argued, there was a knock at the door. "Okay, kids, for Hobo's sake, please try . . . try to be nice to the Buels," Carol said. As she opened the door, Becky and Adam retreated to the kitchen where they could watch from the doorway.

"Hello," Carol said. "I'm Carol Norman. You must be the Buels. Won't you please come in?"

Mrs. Buel, who was tall and skinny and dressed in a once-fashionable black dress with large white polka dots, glanced around the room and kept her nose in the air. Coolly, she said, "Thank you," as the family came inside.

Mr. Buel was plump and had rosy cheeks. His brown and green striped sports jacket was too large and looked silly with his maroon slacks, but he appeared to be cheerful enough—compared to his wife, anyway.

The little girl was plain. The most noticeable thing about her was the spotless navy-blue party dress she was wearing.

Carol led them into the living room and said, "Mr. and Mrs. Buel, this is my husband, Peter, and—Becky, Adam, come here—and these are our children, Becky and Adam. And this is Hobo. Your daughter's name is . . . ?"

Mrs. Buel glared at the homely child and said, "Adele, dear, say 'hello'."

Adele started to curtsy, but Hobo jumped up on her and began licking her face. She tried to push him away, but he persisted and finally knocked her to the floor. "Down, doggie! Down!" she cried.

"The dog certainly doesn't behave very well, does it," Mrs. Buel said sarcastically.

Mr. Buel sighed and said, "It's a dog, Lucille. What do you expect?"

Hobo continued to lick Adele's face, and she continued to say, "Down, doggie."

Adam and Becky stood back in the kitchen doorway.

"Er . . . he's very friendly," Carol said.

"I like him," Adele finally said. She began patting Hobo.

"Adele, dear! Look at your dress! Your beautiful navy-blue dress. That dog sheds!"

"It's a dog," Mr. Buel said. "Dogs shed."

Looking at her dress, Adele said, "I don't like this dress anyway. I like this doggie. Nice doggie." She hugged Hobo.

"Stop!" yelled Mrs. Buel frantically. "Adele, dear, don't do that. It's not sanitary."

Mr. Buel sighed again. "It's a dog, Lucille. Dogs lick."

"I want it! I want the doggie!" whined Adele.

"Oh, brother," Adam mumbled.

Becky, in tears, hid behind the kitchen wall.

Carol, almost in tears herself, said, "Adam, take care of Becky." Then, to Mrs. Buel, she said, "This is all so hard on the children. They love that dog so."

Mrs. Buel studied Hobo and finally said, "How much does it eat?"

Irritated, Peter said, "What? Half a can a day."

Impatiently, Mrs. Buel said, "No . . . I mean, how much does that cost?"

"Oh." Peter glanced at Carol. "Not much. Maybe a quarter."

"And diseases. Does it have any diseases?" Mrs. Buel continued to stare at Hobo, who was still caught in Adele's grip.

"Of course he doesn't have any diseases!" Peter said, more annoyed than ever. "Hobo's a very healthy dog!"

Growing impatient himself, Mr. Buel said, "It's a dog, Lucille. We came to get a dog. What do you expect for free?"

Adele got an even firmer hold on Hobo and screamed, "You promised, you promised me a dog!"

"But, dear," said Mrs. Buel, "we don't know what kind it is or anything about it. It's much bigger than I expected. Wouldn't you like a smaller doggie, Adele, one you could carry around like a dolly?"

"No! I want this one. I want it, I want it!"

"Oh, all right," said Mrs. Buel, sighing. "We'll take it."

Carol, barely able to control her anger, said, "I'm so glad you like Hobo. That's his name. We've . . ."

Mrs. Buel interrupted and said, "Well, we'll certainly change that!"

"I'm going to call it Lassie!" Adele announced.

"Excuse me," Carol said, clearing her throat and glancing at Peter. "As I was saying, we've had so many responses to the ad that we're taking the names of all those families who are interested in adopting Hobo."

Peter had to turn his face to hide the surprised grin.

"And," continued Carol, "we'll go over the list and decide which family we feel will be best for Hobo." She smiled at Becky and Adam who were watching and listening closely. "And we'll let everyone know next week."

"Wait a minute!" Mrs. Buel snarled. "What is this! You don't think we're good enough for that dog?"

Carol winked at Peter and said, "I . . . I didn't say that. But there are others who are also interested."

Mrs. Buel's face turned red as she shook her finger at Carol and said, "You mean you got us all the way over here for nothing?"

Mr. Buel seemed embarrassed as he said, "Lucille, it's just a dog."

"No," Carol said. "Not for nothing. You will be given equal consideration along with the others."

Adele finally released her hold on Hobo and stood up. She jumped up and down and yelled, "I want it now! It's my doggie! I won't go home without it. You promised!"

Carol, carefully controlling her tone of voice, said "Adele, dear, if you are really interested in having Hobo, you should be putting your best foot forward."

Unable to hold off any longer, Peter stepped forward and said, "And one foot after the other leads right to the front door." He took her hand and started toward the door. Then he turned to her parents and said, "It's been so nice meeting you."

Adele shouted and began jumping again. "I won't go

without Lassie! I won't!" Then she bit Peter on the hand.

"Ouch!" He let her hand loose.

Firmly, Carol said, "There's no Lassie here, Adele."

Mrs. Buel took Adele by the hand and said, "Come along, Adele, dear. These people have wasted enough of our time."

Adele stamped her feet again and yelled, "I won't go without a doggie!"

"We'll go straight to the pet store, dear, and get you a nice little doggie," Mrs. Buel said. "That's what I wanted to do all along."

Mr. Buel, trying to speak with some authority, said, "Now, just a minute, Lucille. A dog is a dog. They charge an arm and a leg in those places. This one is free."

"Yeah!" said Adele. "Let's go to the pet store, but I want an ice cream on the way!"

Carol held the door open, and Mrs. Buel walked out with Adele. "Yes, dear," she said. "Don't you worry. We'll find you a *proper* doggie."

Reluctantly, Mr. Buel followed them out, and then he said, "Lucille, you don't know a darn thing about dogs!"

"Don't you use that tone of voice with me, Arnold. Coming here was your idea!"

Carol closed the door and hugged Peter. "Whew!" She sighed as they went back into the living room.

Becky ran to Hobo and said, "Hobo! Hobo!"

"They didn't take him!" Adam yelled, picking Hobo up.

"I wouldn't let that family take Hobo for a million dollars!" Carol said.

13

After the Buels left, Adam and Becky took Hobo to the park. As they played near the stone wall, Adam suddenly noticed Mrs. Baleeka as she sat down on the same bench with Gigi. Again, Gigi was wearing her coat and a pink ribbon. Mrs. Baleeka was wearing her pink costume, too.

"Hey, look!" Adam whispered to Becky. "Get down. Let's watch."

A couple of minutes later, the same strange-looking man walked up to the bench, and this time he sat down. Mrs. Baleeka, looking as bored as ever, stared straight ahead and impatiently tapped her foot as the man patted Gigi and then slipped something under her coat.

"Did you see that?" Adam whispered as the man got up and left. "Did you see that, Becky? That man put something under Gigi's coat. We gotta find out what it is!"

"Yeah," Becky said. Her eyes widened.

"Come on, let's take the short cut and beat her back." Adam grabbed Becky's hand, and with Hobo, they ran back to the apartment building.

They hid between two parked cars. Then, when Mrs. Baleeka and Gigi appeared, Adam said, "Okay, here she comes. Now, don't forget. Try to feel under Gigi's coat." He ducked out of sight.

As Mrs. Baleeka and Gigi got closer, Becky began bouncing a ball off the wall of the building. Then, just as they started to go up the stairs to the stoop, Becky dropped the ball and grabbed at Gigi, but Mrs. Baleeka was too fast. She jerked the leash and pulled the little poodle away.

"Don't you touch Gigi, you horrid child!" snapped the ridiculous-looking woman. "Don't you ever touch her! Can't you read that sign, 'No ballplaying'? If I catch you again, I'll call the police." She stormed into the building as Becky, terrified, stood there.

"Well," said Adam as he and Hobo ran toward her, "did you feel anything?"

"Yeah," Becky said. "Scared."

"I know she was mean to you. But she's mean to everybody. Couldn't you feel anything under Gigi's coat?"

Becky hugged Hobo, who jumped up on her, and said, "She wouldn't even let me get close."

Adam, trying to hide his disappointment, said, "Well, at least we know she met with that same weird man. I

94

bet there'll be some action soon. Want to come with me down to the basement tonight?"

"No," Becky said firmly.

By the time dinner was over that evening, Becky had changed her mind, and she went down to the cellar with Adam. First, they checked an old file cabinet that Mr. Baleeka kept down there by the washers and dryers, but it was locked. Then they looked in some of the old crates and trunks that were stacked all over the basement, but there was nothing but junk in them.

"See," Adam said after they had snooped around for several minutes, "there's nothing to be afraid of."

"Yeah?" said Becky. "Then how come I'm so scared?"

" 'Cause you're younger than me, Becky, but you're brave. I gotta hand it to you, you're brave."

Becky was pleased, and she followed Adam to the door with the fake padlock on it. As they got closer, they suddenly heard voices. "Shhh!" Adam whispered. He looked through the keyhole and saw Mr. Baleeka and Bill inside. They listened and heard Mr. Baleeka say, "No lettuce, no ice!"

"Hey, man," said Bill, "relax. You got Marko's word."

"Listen," Mr. Baleeka said angrily, "the only good word Marko's got is C-A-S-H. Now get out and don't come back till you can make the deal."

"Hurry!" Adam whispered. "Here they come!" He grabbed Becky's hand, and they scrambled behind the trash cans.

"Boy, that was close!" Becky said after the men had gone up in the elevator.

"Yeah, but did you hear what they said?"

"You mean about lettuce and ice?"

"Yeah," Adam said, climbing out from behind the cans. "Why would anybody want lettuce and ice down here?"

Becky shrugged and said, "Grown-ups are crazy."

Upstairs, in the living room, Peter and Carol were discussing Hobo again.

"Look, Carol, we've tried friends and friends of friends, we've put an ad in the paper, and still no luck. People who want a dog go to the A.S.P.C.A. They're set up to handle pet adoption."

Carol sank down in the sofa and said, "And you know as well as I do that two or three hundred pets are destroyed every day in this city because they can't find homes for them. If a dog isn't adopted in seventy-two hours, it's put to sleep. The A.S.P.C.A. do the best they can, but that's not good enough."

Peter paced back and forth. Finally, he said, "Carol, our September and October rent checks still haven't been cashed. By the end of the week there will be an eviction notice on our door. And, unfortunately, the law is on Baleeka's side."

"Oh, I wish we'd never taken Hobo," Carol said as she nervously pulled at a lock of hair.

"What!" Peter stopped pacing. "And left him in that raccoon trap?"

"No, no, of course not. It's just that . . . I don't know. There must be a way to keep Hobo."

Hobo heard his name and jumped up onto her lap.

"Hey, what's wrong?" asked Adam as he and Becky came back inside from the basement.

"I'm afraid we're at the end of our rope, kids," Peter said. "We can't keep Hobo any longer."

"We'll lose the apartment," Carol added, wiping tears away.

Adam stood motionless and said, "Let's move then."

"We can't afford to move," his father said. "You know that. But there's one last chance for Hobo. There's something called the *City Shelter Program for Animals*, the C.S.P.A. They'll take a pet and put it up for adoption. People looking for a pet go there."

"But," said Carol bitterly, "if nobody takes it within three days, it's put to sleep, just the same as with the A.S.P.C.A."

"Oh, no!" Becky began to cry.

"You wouldn't take Hobo there!" Adam looked at his father as though he were a traitor.

Peter shrugged and said, "We don't have much choice, Adam. We've tried everything else. I think we should take Hobo to the C.S.P.A. this Friday, and give him the whole weekend for his chances at adoption."

Becky threw herself down on the sofa and hugged Hobo. "Hobo, Hobo!" she cried.

"Dad, please, can't we wait a little longer? Please!" Adam pleaded.

"I know how it hurts," his father said, sympathetically, "but the sooner, the better. This waiting, hoping for some other solution . . . it's too hard on all of us." Then, firmly, he said, "I'll meet you out front after school Friday in the car, and we'll all go together."

"Yeah, that's just great!" Adam went into the bedroom and slammed the door.

The next few days were the most miserable Becky and Adam had ever known. They gave up trying to play detective, but then on Friday after school, before their father showed up with the car, Adam said, "Mom, I'm going to take Hobo for one last walk."

"Okay," she said, "but don't take too long. There's nothing more . . . Oh, Adam, I forgot the laundry in the drier. Please take it out for me."

"Oh, okay," Adam grumbled as he snapped the leash to Hobo's collar. "Come on, boy."

When the elevator door opened in the basement, Hobo growled, and Adam saw Mr. Baleeka looking at some papers in his file cabinet.

"Get away! Get that dog outta here!" yelled Mr. Baleeka. He kicked at Hobo and shoved the papers back inside the top drawer.

Adam tugged at the leash and said, "Hush, Hobo. Sorry, Mr. Baleeka."

"Yeah," said the landlord, heading for the elevator, "you'll be even sorrier when I slap that eviction notice on your door. Either you or that mutt goes."

After Mr. Baleeka got in the elevator, Hobo began sniffing around the file cabinet. In his haste, Mr. Baleeka had forgotten to close and lock it.

While Adam took the laundry out of the drier, Hobo pulled at the handle of the bottom drawer, and it slid open.

"Hey, what are you doing?" Adam called at Hobo.

Then he saw the open drawer. He glanced around the dimly lit cellar to make certain no one was coming, and then he began to look through the papers in the drawer. Mostly there were just old bills and canceled checks, but then he spotted an old foreign passport in the back of the drawer. He opened it and saw a picture of a younger Mr. Baleeka, but that wasn't the name on the passport. It was *Joseph Malinetti.*

"Good boy, good boy, Hobo!" said Adam as he put the passport back and closed the drawer. "This may be just what we need." He grabbed the laundry, and together he and Hobo ran for the elevator.

When they got back upstairs, Carol was trying to comfort Becky, who was crying.

"Mom! Mom!" yelled Adam, throwing the laundry on the sofa. "Guess what! Mr. Baleeka isn't really Mr. Baleeka!"

"What are you talking about, Adam? Just take Hobo down to the car. Your father's waiting."

"But, Mom! I found this old foreign passport of Mr. Baleeka's, but with a different name. That means he's a crook, or trying to hide something, doesn't it?"

Carol, who was frantically trying to get both kids to move, said, "What on earth are you talking about?"

"Mom, listen. Mr. Baleeka left his file cabinet open, and there was this picture of him when he was younger, but with a different name."

Carol opened the front door and tried to push both kids out. "Adam, move! Becky!" As they walked toward the elevator, she said, "Lots of people changed their names when they came to this country. It doesn't mean a thing.

Darned elevator! Let's walk. We have to hurry. Your father says the sooner we get there, the better chance Hobo will have for adoption.

"But, Mumma!" Becky cried.

14

Peter was waiting for them in the car. Becky was still crying and tugging at her mother's dress. "Come on, we've got to get going," Peter yelled.

"Dad, couldn't I take Hobo for one last walk?" Adam asked. "Just to the corner."

"No, we have to get there before they close."

"Oh, Peter, one last walk, please. I told him . . ."

"Thanks, Mom!" Without waiting for his father's response, Adam ran down the street with Hobo.

"Popi! Popi!" sobbed Becky, as she got into the car. "Don't take Hobo to the shelter. Please! They'll put him to sleep forever, you know they will. Please don't take him, please!"

Carol got in next to Peter and said, "This is insane. There must be some other way."

"What can I say?" Peter said, sighing. "We've tried. Oh, Becky, please stop crying."

"No, no, no!" Becky began hitting him with her fists.

"Becky, stop!"

A truck behind them honked, and as Peter pulled next to a fire hydrant to let it pass, he said, "Where's Adam? He said 'just to the corner'."

Adam and Hobo ducked into an alley and took the shortcut to the park. As they ran, Adam crouched down. When they got to the park, he looked around to make certain there was nobody around who knew him. Panting, he said, "Come on, Hobo, we've got to go farther." He pointed. "Over there where all the big trees and bushes are."

When they got to the boat pond, Adam saw a hotdog vendor who was just closing his umbrella for the night. Quickly, he reached into his pockets for some change. "We've got just enough for two," he said to Hobo. He turned to the vendor. "Please, may we have two?"

The vendor grumbled and said, "Okay, kid, but I've already put the mustard away."

Glancing around, Adam said, "That's all right. Don't need mustard." He paid the vendor and took the hot dogs. Then they ran into the wooded area. "This should do," he said to Hobo.

They sat down in the grass, and Adam gave one of the hot dogs to Hobo, who dropped the bun and quickly gobbled the meat down. Adam patted him and said, "This is all we can get, Hobo. I don't know what we're gonna do about breakfast. But I do know nobody's gonna put you to sleep."

Hobo watched Adam hopefully as he ate. "You're still hungry, aren't you, boy? Here." He gave Hobo the rest of his hot dog. "I'm not hungry anyway," he said.

Hobo gulped down the meat. Then he started chasing a squirrel. It ran up a tree, and Hobo barked furiously.

Adam looked around again, but didn't see anyone. It was beginning to get dark, and he felt chilly. Where are we going to sleep tonight? he wondered. As he thought, he heard a scratching sound. He turned and saw two large gray rats nibbling on the bread. Terrified, he got up and ran to Hobo. He clipped the leash to Hobo's collar and said, "Come on, boy. We've gotta find a place for the night."

As they walked, Adam said, "Hobo, from here on, you and me are going to be together." Hobo wagged his tail and licked Adam's hand.

Suddenly Hobo began to growl.

Startled, Adam said, "What is it, Hobo? What's the matter?"

Hobo growled again. Then he turned and looked up a hill behind them.

Adam turned, too, and as he did, he saw a pack of stray dogs. They were barking and running toward them. "Come on, Hobo, run!"

They ran on through the trees, and then suddenly there was a high stone wall in front of them. "Go home! Get! Go home!" Adam shouted at the dogs. He picked up a dead branch and hit a big dog with it. The dog yelped and started to retreat, but the others were still charging.

Adam threw the branch. Then he picked up a rock and threw it at another dog. The dog moaned, and when it stopped, the others did, too. "Hurry, Hobo, we've got to get up here," he said, trying to get a handhold in the wall.

As the dogs began barking again, Adam got to the top of the wall. He pulled on the leash, and Hobo scrambled up after him. From the top, Adam threw more sticks and loose rocks, and finally the dogs turned and loped away.

"That was too close," Adam said, hugging Hobo. "But at least we're safe—for now."

They climbed down from the wall and walked on, and as they did, it got darker and darker in the park. Finally, as city lights began to glow in the sky above the trees, Adam saw a clump of evergreen bushes and said, "Come on, Hobo. This looks like as good as place as any to spend the night."

With Hobo leading the way, Adam crawled under the bushes. And then he saw a large refrigerator carton. "Hey," he said, feeling better. "Indians on the trail never had it this good." He crawled inside and said, "Come on, Hobo."

Adam leaned against the end of the carton and Hobo snuggled up next to him. "Not bad, huh?" he said.

"Who needs the Baleekas' old apartment? But I do miss Mom and Dad, don't you, Hobo? I even miss Becky."

Hobo jumped up and began to growl.

"What is it, boy? Shush!" Frightened, he listened. Something was moving through the bushes outside the carton. Twigs snapped. Terrified, Adam closed his eyes and hugged Hobo.

Suddenly he heard a deep voice say, "What are you doing in my house?"

Hobo barked, and Adam slowly opened his eyes. A large young black man with a full beard was looking inside the carton. "Er . . . who . . . I . . . I didn't know this was your house. And we didn't have any other place to go."

"It's all right, pup," the man said. "I won't hurt you." He gave Hobo a pat on the head, and the barking stopped. "I'm sorry to hear you didn't have any place to go," he said gently. He grinned and said, "Mind if I come in?" He reached into his jacket pocket and pulled out a candle. When he lit it, Adam could see he looked friendly.

Grinning back and relaxing some, Adam said, "Of course I don't mind. It's your house." He and Hobo scooted back to the end.

"What's your name?" the man asked as he sat down near the opening.

"It's . . . my name's Adam."

The man reached to shake hands and said, "Glad to meet you. My name's Kenneth."

Hobo walked over to Kenneth and began sniffing at his pockets.

"Hey, did you guys skip supper tonight?" Kenneth asked.

"We had a couple of hot dogs. Actually, he ate one and a half. He's always hungry."

Kenneth laughed and pulled a large hero sandwich from his jacket pocket. He broke it into three sections. "Here, be my guest," he said, handing part to Adam and part to Hobo, who gobbled it down, bread and all this time.

"Sure you don't mind?" Adam asked, taking the offering.

"Go ahead. The panhandling was pretty good today," Kenneth said as he took a bite.

"Thanks." Adam watched him in the flickering candlelight. "What's panhandling?"

"Heh, heh," Kenneth chuckled. "Panhandling is requesting a handout from one's more affluent brothers. As long as other people are good at making money, I let 'em do it. All I ask is for a little on the side." He chewed the last bite and said, "It beats welfare. At least I'm my own man."

"You mean you're a hobo!" Adam said.

Kenneth let some wax drip onto the carton, and then he set the candle in place. "People call me a lot of things," he said.

Adam scratched behind Hobo's ears and said, "His name's Hobo. I rescued him from a raccoon trap."

Kenneth stretched out along one side of the carton and said, "Okay, how about you filling me in on the whys and wherefores, and how come you're paying me this visit and have no place to go." He gently patted Adam on the shoulder and said, "Start with the raccoon trap, if you'd like."

"Well," said Adam, yawning, "you see, I'm interested in Indians, and I was following these animal tracks when I heard . . ."

As Adam told his story, Hobo fell asleep between them, and the candle burned down and began to flicker rapidly. Outside the dim sounds of traffic could be heard in the distance.

"Anyway," Adam said, yawning and blinking his eyes, "I figured with Mr. Baleeka changing his name and everything, we'd have something on him and he'd let us keep Hobo. But Mom says lots of people change their names. So instead of taking Hobo to the shelter, I ran away. I'm not gonna let anybody put this dog to sleep."

"Yeah," Kenneth said, sympathetically, "I can see how you feel. But, you know, from what you've said, this Baleeka character sounds like a pretty shady type. Now, this other cat, the one who was slipping something to the poodle, think back on it . . . was there anything different in the situation? I mean like, when he did and when he didn't?"

Still yawning, Adam thought. Then he said, "I don't think so. No, wait. The first time when he stopped, Gigi had a pink ribbon on. The second time, when he passed by, she had a blue ribbon. And the third time, when he stopped again, she had the pink ribbon on."

Kenneth nodded, knowingly. "Uh-huh. There, you see! The ribbon was the signal to make contact or not. And that *lettuce* and *ice* you've been wondering about . . . well, that's just jive crook talk for *money* and *jewels*.

107

Sounds to me like this Baleeka cat—this Malinetti—is a fence."

"A what?" asked Adam.

"A fence. He's the middleman between the robbers and the eventual buyers of the stolen merchandise. He's called a fence because he separates one from the other and acts as a barrier to the police who are trying to apprehend . . ." He paused. Adam was sound asleep.

Kenneth blew out what was left of the candle, and as he tried to make himself comfortable in the little space that was left, he said, "Gotta get a guest room one of these days."

15

Early the next morning, Kenneth crept quietly from the carton. Once outside, he stretched and twisted his body, trying to work out the stiffness from his cramped sleeping position. Then he crawled through the evergreen bushes and walked toward the boat pond, where he saw a policeman walking and twirling his nightstick.

"Morning, Janaki," Kenneth said. "I think I've got some business for you." He stretched and twisted some more.

Officer Janaki grinned and said, "What's the matter, Kenneth? Aren't those accommodations posh enough for you anymore?"

Still twisting, Kenneth said, "It's about time to go

south. But what I wanted to talk to you about, and why I slept like a pretzel last night, is I've got guests."

Officer Janaki stopped twirling the nightstick and said, "That's your affair."

"Don't think so," Kenneth said seriously. "The guests are a boy named Adam Norman and a dog named Hobo." He bent down and touched his toes.

"How about that," the policeman said. "Missing persons' file. Came in last night. Where are they?"

Kenneth pointed toward the evergreens, and they walked in that direction.

"Is that so?" Kenneth said, smiling. "Also, you wouldn't have anyone on the *Wanted* list named Joseph Malinetti, would you?"

"Kenneth, sometimes I think half of the people in this city are on that *Wanted* list. But I can check it out."

They got to the evergreens and Kenneth said, "This kid is a junior detective. Hear him out." Then he yelled, "Hey, Adam! Rise and shine."

Adam and Hobo emerged from the carton. Wiping sleep from his eyes, Adam said, "Where are you?"

"Over here!"

Hobo ran through the evergreens and jumped up on Kenneth. Adam crawled through and said, "Good morning." But then he saw the policeman and frowned. "Oh, no. What are you doing here?" He felt hurt and angry.

"Take it easy, Adam," Kenneth said. "He's my friend, Officer Janaki. He wants to help you. And if he helps out stray people like me, for sure he'd help a marvelous stray dog like Hobo."

Officer Janaki put his arm around Adam and said,

"I'll try to help you. Come with me, and we'll tell your story to the sergeant at the precinct. Kenneth says you've done some pretty fancy police work on your own. And I know your parents will be happy to hear that you're okay. They were pretty upset last night."

"Yeah, I bet they were," Adam said. He turned to Kenneth and said, "Thanks for the hero and the place to sleep."

Kenneth grinned and said, "Don't mention it. My house is your house."

Adam walked toward the park exit with the policeman, and Hobo followed, after licking Kenneth goodbye.

"So long," Adam said, waving.

"Good luck," Kenneth called.

After Adam told the whole story, the precinct sergeant called Carol and Peter, and Officer Janaki took Hobo and Adam home.

Becky met them at the door, and as she hugged Hobo, she yelled, "Mumma! Popi! They're home!"

Carol ran to Adam and hugged and kissed him. "Oh, Adam, you're all right. We were so worried." She held him close.

Peter shook hands with Officer Janaki, and the policeman said, "Your Adam's quite a kid." He winked at Adam.

"We'd sure like to meet the man who found Adam," Peter said, "and thank him personally."

Officer Janaki grinned and said, "I'm sure that can be arranged."

"And thank you, too, officer," Carol said, finally releasing Adam. "It was kind of you to bring him home."

"And Hobo, too," Becky said. They rolled on the floor together.

"Don't mention it." Officer Janaki shook Adam's hand and said, "Good luck. I hope things work out." He turned to Peter and said, "I'll ask Kenneth, the man who found Adam, to stop by around . . . three this afternoon?"

"That'll be fine," Peter said.

As Officer Janaki left, Adam said, "So long."

Carol hugged him again and said, "We were so worried."

"Tell us about it." Peter hugged him, too. "Where did you go? How did you meet Kenneth?"

"Do you think he'd like a pineapple upside-down cake?" Carol asked. "I'd like to make something for him."

"He likes hero sandwiches," Adam said.

Adam told them the whole story, and afterwards Carol made the pineapple upside-down cake. Later, as they were all talking in the kitchen, there was a knock at the door.

"Peter, could you get it?" Carol asked. "I have to at least splash some cold water on my face." She looked at Adam. "Needless to say, we didn't sleep last night."

Peter opened the door and Kenneth was standing there, grinning and holding a bunch of flowers. "The panhandling was pretty good today, so I brought you these." He handed them to Peter.

"How nice! Thank you," Peter said. "Come on in."

Kenneth looked around the room. Then he sniffed and said, "Mmmmm, what is that delightful aroma?"

Leading him toward the sofa, Peter said, "Hope you like pineapple upside-down cake. My wife just baked it."

Kenneth sat down and said, "Homemade anything has got to be one of my favorites."

"Look what Kenneth brought," Peter said as Carol and Adam came into the living room."

"What a lovely thing to do." She smelled the flowers.

"Hi, Kenneth," Adam said, grinning. "Welcome to *my* house." He pointed to Becky, who was still playing with Hobo, and said, "This is my sister."

"Good to meet . . ."

He was interrupted by a knock on the door.

"Becky, go see who that is," Carol said. Turning to Kenneth, she said, "I can't tell you how grateful we are."

"They were just lucky," Kenneth said. "They picked the right carton."

"Honey, what'll we do with these flowers?" Peter asked.

Just then Hobo began barking, and Becky yelled, "Mumma!"

Mr. Baleeka walked into the living room, waving a paper. "Glad to see you're enjoying yourselves," he said sarcastically. "This is the last party you'll have here. I'm serving you personally with this eviction notice. You've broken your lease." He slapped the document down on Carol's desk. Then, noticing Kenneth and eyeing his tattered clothing, he said, "Who's he?"

Kenneth stood up and hovered over Mr. Baleeka. "Me?" he said, in a gruff tone of voice. "I'm thinking of subletting this place since the Normans can't keep it."

"What!" said Mr. Baleeka, backing away from Kenneth.

There was another knock at the door. And then a shout: "Open up in the name of the law!"

The Normans and Kenneth hurried toward the front door, and Mr. Baleeka rushed into the kitchen toward the back door.

Adam opened the door, and two policemen were standing there. One said, "I have a warrant for the arrest of Joseph Malinetti, alias Joseph Baleeka. Is he in your apartment, ma'am?"

"He certainly is," Carol said happily. "Come in."

They crowded into the living room, and Peter said, "He was here."

Hobo began sniffing around. Then he ran to the kitchen where the door was open a crack.

"Here! Here!" yelled Adam, following Hobo. "He got out this way." He opened the door all the way and caught a glimpse of Mr. Baleeka running down the back stairs. Hobo took off after him, and Adam and the others followed.

The policemen caught up with Adam on the stairs, and one said, "Let us go first, son. He may be dangerous."

"Yeah!" Adam yelled as they edged past him. "He's got a gun."

Hobo was barking on the next floor and chasing after Mr. Baleeka.

"Stop! Stop in the name of the law!" one of the policemen yelled.

An apartment door opened and an old woman, holding a partially completed sampler, said, "What's all this ruckus about?"

Peter ran past her and yelled, "We're after the Baleekas."

"Eldridge!" shouted the woman, dropping the sampler. "Come on! They're after the Baleekas!" She joined the chase, and an old man, carrying a newspaper, ran out the door after her. "Yippee!" he yelled. "We're finally going to get the Baleekas!"

More apartment doors opened, and more tenants joined the chase.

Down another flight of stairs ran Mr. Baleeka with Hobo at his heels. "Stick with him, Hobo!" Adam yelled from above.

"I never thought I'd see the day!" shouted another old lady who hadn't had time to put her false teeth in.

Eldridge passed her on the next floor and said, "Always knew he was a crook, that Simon Legree!"

"He never did fix our sink!" someone else shouted.

"Or our radiator!" came another voice.

"Wait till I get my hands on him!" said a big, burly man who ran out barefoot and wrapped in a bath towel.

Mr. Baleeka finally made it to the basement, and he quickly unlocked the door with the fake padlock. Hobo nipped at him, but he kicked at the dog and slammed the door.

When the others got there, Hobo was sniffing around the door.

"Hobo, Hobo! Where are you, boy?" Adam yelled, trying to adjust his eyes to the dark cellar. Hobo growled and then began barking again.

"Which way'd he go?" asked another voice.

"Where is he?"

"Must have gotten out the back."

People were looking behind garbage cans, trunks, old crates—everything. The policemen were standing at the open cellar door that led to the alley.

"Come back!" Adam yelled. "He's in here!"

The whole group ran to Adam, and one of the policemen said, "Where is he, son?"

"See! Where Hobo's sniffing. He must be in there."

Both policemen drew their pistols, and one shouted, "Everybody else stay back!"

They approached the door, and then one said, "Naw, this one's locked from the outside."

"No!" Adam said, running toward them. "It's fake!"

He pulled on the door.

"Well, I'll be! Okay, stand back." The policemen entered the room, and Hobo ran in with them.

"Hobo! Come back!" Adam yelled.

"Joseph Malinetti, surrender in the name of the law!" yelled one of the policemen.

There was no answer as the policemen shone their flashlights into the dark corners. The room was dingy, and even more crates and trunks were stored at one end. But Mr. Baleeka was not there.

As the policemen turned to leave the room, Adam said, "Wait! That trunk! Hobo's sniffing that trunk. I bet you'll find him in there."

Cautiously, with their pistols still drawn, the policemen approached the trunk and quickly opened it.

But the trunk was empty.

"Blast it!" said one of the policemen. "Looks like we've lost him. He must have gotten out and ducked into one of the stores down the block. Come on, let's go."

As the policemen, followed by all the people, went back to the door that led to the alley, Adam went up to Hobo, who was still sniffing around the trunk. "Hobo," he said, annoyed, "what are you doing?"

Hobo scratched at the trunk and tried to move it away from the wall. He was growling.

"Hey!" Adam shouted. "Here!"

One of the policemen came back into the dark room and flashed his light on Adam and Hobo. "What are you doing in here?"

"Look," Adam said, pointing at Hobo. "He's trying to move that trunk."

Cautiously, the policeman pushed the trunk away. Behind it there was an old coal chute. Hobo jumped into it and began barking furiously. The policeman shone his light into it and said, "Good work."

Mr. Baleeka was lying in the chute, and Hobo was tugging on his pant leg, trying to pull him out. In the light, the policeman could see several plastic bags of jewelry.

"All right, Malinetti, come on out with your hands up."

"Rotten mutt," Mr. Baleeka grumbled as he crawled out and raised his hands.

The other policeman came into the room, and all of the others watched from outside the door. As the officers handcuffed Mr. Baleeka, Adam crawled up the chute with Hobo, and together they brought out three bags of jewelry. "Look what was up there!"

One of the policemen flashed his light on Adam, who was covered with soot and coal dust, and said, "Jewelry from the *El Doro* robbery, I'll bet."

The other officer said, "Now I know why he was known as the biggest bag man in town. We've been looking for him for years."

As the one policeman shoved Mr. Baleeka through the door, Adam gave two bags of jewels to the other. Hobo still had the third bag in his mouth. "Drop it. Hobo, drop it!" Adam commanded.

But Hobo wouldn't drop it.

The officer laughed and said, "I don't blame him. He deserves a reward. In fact, you all do, and you'll get it . . . a new landlord. Where this one's going, he won't bother you anymore."

"Come on, Hobo," Adam commanded again. "Let me have it." Finally Hobo dropped the bag. Then he ran toward Mr. Baleeka and gave him a farewell growl.

"He's some dog," said one of the policemen, patting Hobo on the head. "We could use a whole kennel of dogs like him."

The crowd followed as the policemen led Mr. Baleeka upstairs to the first floor and to the patrol car outside. "Get moving, Malinetti. You can join your wife and your buddy, Bill, in the car."

Everyone cheered as the car drove off.

Back in the apartment, Adam and Becky hugged

and praised Hobo, who was sharing a piece of pineapple upside-down cake with Kenneth. Peter winked at Carol and said, "Looks as though our summer dog is here to stay."

Songs from the Motion Picture

"Running Free"
"Hobo and Me"

RUNNING FREE

lyrics: B. Tarallo

music: R. Lamont / B. Tarallo

Home is any — where I lie me down, any-where I hang my hat. From the sunrise, following moon-down, I'll be running free — I feel like I'm ten feet high, & every cloud is ben-ding down to say Hello. One with the wind & sky I'm — run-ning

soak up all that sun _____ you'll see a brand new day — has just begun _____ , running free _____

HOBO and ME

lyrics: R. Lamont

music: { R. Lamont
{ B. Tarallo

1) Hobo & me, we got a good thing go-ing, to-gether

2) Hobo & me, you can ge-neral-ly find us, to-gether

(1) He knows what I'm thinking, be-fore I can speak, he don't

(2) It's good to have a friend who will stick by you, when you're

1) mind when I sing off — key

2) sailing on stormy

fine.

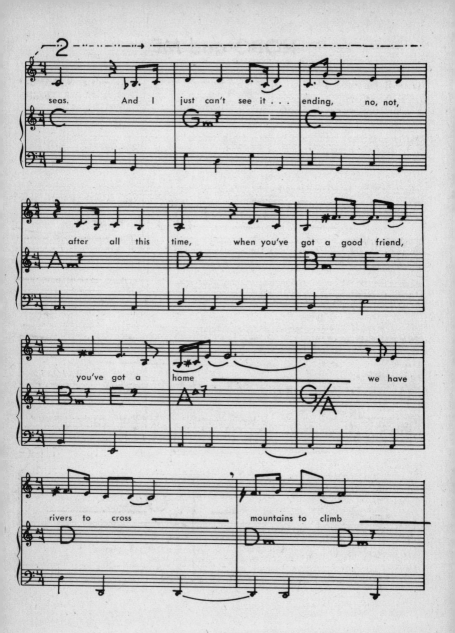

but if you're gone _____ who will light the way _____ who will share the

D.C. al fine.

lucky days

3)
Hobo & me, we got a good thing going together.
He knows what I'm thinking, before I can speak . . .
Understanding, comes naturally. . . .

4)
Hobo & me, inseparably, together.

My best friend & me, we have a kind of love

You don't let go of, easily . . .